always, forever

ALSO BY NANCY OHLIN

BEAUTY

always, forever

NANCY OHLIN

PREVIOUSLY TITLED *THORN ABBEY*

SIMON PULSE

NEW YORK   LONDON   TORONTO   SYDNEY   NEW DELHI

This book is a work of fiction. Any references to historical events, real people, or real places are used fictitiously. Other names, characters, places, and events are products of the author's imagination, and any resemblance to actual events or places or persons, living or dead, is entirely coincidental.

SIMON PULSE

An imprint of Simon & Schuster Children's Publishing Division

1230 Avenue of the Americas, New York, NY 10020

First Simon Pulse paperback edition April 2014

Text copyright © 2013 by Nancy Ohlin

Cover photograph copyright © 2014 by Clayton Bastiani/Trevillion Images

Cover design by Jessica Handelman

Previously titled *Thorn Abbey*

Also available in a Simon Pulse hardcover edition titled *Thorn Abbey*.

For information about special discounts for bulk purchases, please contact Simon & Schuster Special Sales at 1-866-506-1949 or business@simonandschuster.com.

The Simon & Schuster Speakers Bureau can bring authors to your live event. For more information or to book an event contact the Simon & Schuster Speakers Bureau at 1-866-248-3049 or visit our website at www.simonspeakers.com.

Interior design by Angela Goddard and Regina Flath

The text of this book was set in Berling LT Std.

Manufactured in the United States of America

10 9 8 7 6 5 4 3 2 1

The Library of Congress has cataloged the hardcover edition as follows:

Ohlin, Nancy.

[Thorn Abbey]

Always, forever / Nancy Ohlin. — First Simon Pulse paperback edition.

p. cm.

Originally published in 2013 under title: Thorn Abbey.

Summary: When Tess transfers to New England's premier boarding school, Thorn Abbey, she quickly falls for mysterious, brooding Max, but Max is still mourning the death of his girlfriend, Becca, and Becca's ghost is not quite ready to let him go.

[1. Boarding schools—Fiction. 2. Schools—Fiction. 3. Ghosts—Fiction. 4. Dating (Social customs)—Fiction. 5. New England—Fiction.] I. Title.

PZ7.O41404Al 2014   [Fic]—dc23   2013044996

ISBN 978-1-4424-6486-5 (*Thorn Abbey* hc)

ISBN 978-1-4424-6487-2 (pbk)

ISBN 978-1-4814-1586-6 (eBook)

For Jens

PROLOGUE

THE DREAM IS ALWAYS THE SAME. I AM WALKING DOWN THE
path, the one that winds through the woods by Thorn Abbey
and leads down to the beach. The air is cool and wet with rain,
and my footsteps are light on the carpet of brown fallen leaves
as I hurry down to the place where I know he is waiting for
me. My cheeks are cold, and my heavy wool sweater scratches
against my skin, but I don't care because I can already feel his
strong arms around my body and his warm lips against mine.

And then I am at the bottom of the hill. The beach rises
above the horizon, endless and gray. Suddenly I feel exposed.
Frightened. The air is different here: bigger, less forgiving. It
smells like the sea and salt and dead things.

I move closer to the water. A wave rushes up to my boots

and then snakes away, leaving two identical dark stains. I shudder against the chill and look around. Where is he, and why is he late?

Another wave comes up, more imposing than the last, and I step back. But the wave doesn't retreat. It keeps rising toward me, not cresting or breaking. I cry out and stumble backward. The wave grows larger, more menacing, finally overtaking me and sucking me into its icy deep.

Hands, fingers, hair. *Her* hands, her fingers, her hair. They wrap around me, colder than death, and pull me under as I scream. Her face—her beautiful, perfect face that he loved with a passion he will never feel for me—is the last thing I see as my lungs fill with the brackish water and I black out into the nothingness, still calling out his name in vain.

❧ PART ONE ❧

1.

"TESS, THIS IS DEVON MCCAIN. SHE'LL BE YOUR ROOMMATE. Devon, this is Tess Szekeres. She's a sophomore."

The house counselor, Mrs. Frith, moves aside as she makes the introductions and waves me into my new room. I enter, hesitating in the doorway as two enormous emerald eyes size me up.

"Hi, Tess! Welcome to Thorn Abbey!" Devon steps forward and gives me a quick, fierce hug. She is tall, maybe five ten, and reminds me of an Amazon warrior. Her long, silky black hair looks striking against her crisp white blouse and plaid school jumper.

"I'll leave you to unpack and get settled," Mrs. Frith says to me. "Devon is a junior. From Boston. She's been here since ninth grade, so she can fill you in on anything you need to know."

"Yeah, like all the best places on campus to get high and make out," Devon says merrily.

My cheeks grow hot as I wait for Mrs. Frith to start yelling or give Devon a detention or something. But instead, she laughs. "Good one, Devon. Don't forget the Welcome Tea at four, in the downstairs parlors. See you girls then."

"Lipton's and stale scones. Can't wait." Devon closes the door after Mrs. Frith and turns to me with a dazzling smile. She has perfect teeth—braces, obviously—and I instinctively clamp my mouth shut. "I thought she'd *never* leave. Come on, show me the clothes you brought. I saved you the good closet."

"Um, thanks. I didn't bring . . . that is, I wasn't sure what I was supposed to . . ."

My voice drifts as I picture my wardrobe, Old Navy circa 2010, folded neatly in my one suitcase. I glance around the room, which is so much bigger than my own at home. Devon, who must have arrived on the early side of check-in, has already taken possession of her half. She's hung framed posters on the yellow-rose wallpaper: a *Vogue* cover from the sixties, an ad for a German production of the opera *Aida*, and photos of Billie Holiday and Amy Winehouse. Her desk is cluttered with makeup, tampons, an iPod, a white laptop, and what look like birth control pills. There is a purple silk quilt on her bed that looks impossibly glamorous.

Devon plops down on the quilt and kicks off her ballerina flats. She grabs a bottle of nail polish from her nightstand and starts painting her toenails. The way she is sitting, I can just make out a tattoo on her left thigh—a flower?—and a sliver of her black lace panties. I look away.

"Soooo. What is that, Greek?" she asks me.

"What?"

"Your name. Sounds Greek."

"Actually, it's Hungarian. My family's a mix of Hungarian, Swedish, Chinese, Dutch, and a few other things."

"Wow. Mine are, like, straight Irish American. My dad's ancestors were potato farmers from Galway. My nana on my mom's side was an opera singer from Dublin. I'm boring, compared to you."

"I don't think so." I can't imagine Devon ever being boring.

"Where did you transfer from?"

"You mean, what school? Avery Park."

"Never heard of it. Oh my God, is that one of those hippie prep schools where you grow organic vegetables and worship Gaia the earth goddess?"

"No, it's just a regular high school. Like a normal public school. It's in Avery Park, New York, near Albany."

"Oh?" Devon raises one eyebrow. "Well, you're going to love it here. Private school is soooo much better than public school."

"I know. That's why my mom made me apply, because my classes weren't challenging enough and because—"

Devon shakes her head. "No, you idiot, not the classes! I meant the other stuff. You can get away with *anything* in private school."

I stare at her. I'm not sure what to say.

"You have a lot to learn, Young Apprentice," Devon says, smiling her dazzling smile again "Unpack your crap. Then I'll take you on the unofficial tour."

2.

HOW CAN I DESCRIBE THORN ABBEY? IT IS LIKE SOMETHING out of Jane Austen or Harry Potter or a fairy tale. The main building, Lanyon Hall, is an enormous gray stone mansion, practically a castle. It has turrets and towers and tall arched windows that overlook the wide, grassy quadrangle. Or "quad," as Devon calls it. There are gardens everywhere, including flower gardens and herb gardens and even a Shakespeare garden. On the north face of the quad are dorms, including mine, Kerrith Hall. On the south face are more dorms as well as the music and art studios.

To the east is the ocean. It's hard to see it from the quad or anywhere on the ground level because it's beyond a dense forest and below a sharp cliff. But from the higher floors of Lanyon or Kerrith or any other building, there is an amazing view. It is windy today, so the waters are dark and choppy, with a grid of tiny whitecaps that seem almost motionless from a distance.

I think about home. The little ranch house with the scrubby, overgrown lawn. The dying strip mall where my mom and I do our grocery shopping. And of course, Avery Park High, which looks like a massive cinder-block prison in the middle of a bombed-out cornfield. I can still picture the painted metal signs out front: HOME OF THE FIGHTING SPARTANS! and DRUG-FREE GUN-FREE SCHOOL ZONE.

I'm not in Avery Park anymore.

By the time Devon and I arrive at the Welcome Tea, twenty minutes late, she has already shown me the best places to get high and make out, as promised—even though there is less than a zero percent chance that I will ever need to know these things. She has also explained a number of what she called "survival strategies," like how to stay out past the nightly curfew and score food when the dining halls are closed.

Dozens of girls are gathered in the Kerrith parlors. Some of them are dressed in the school uniform, like Devon. The rest are in miniskirts and stylish tops with fancy sandals. I feel dumb in my wrinkled black T-shirt and jeans, which is what I wore on the long, long bus ride from Albany. I hover way in the back, by the antique doors painted with medieval knights and maidens. Parents were on campus when I first arrived, but they seem to be long gone now.

If there was a welcome speech, Devon and I must have missed it. Mrs. Frith is at the refreshment table cutting into a coffee cake, and the girls stand around in tight clusters: talking, laughing, sipping tea from gold and white porcelain cups. Devon grabs my wrist and drags me over to a small group.

"Hey, tramps! Meet Tess," Devon says. "Tess, this is Priscilla, Elinor, and Yoonie. They have a triplet on our floor."

"Hi," I say, forcing a smile.

I can feel three pairs of eyes giving me the once-over. They all seem to linger on my blue flip-flops and unpolished toenails. "Hey," a pretty strawberry blonde with a Southern accent—Priscilla?—says. "Welcome to Kerrith! This is *the* most awesome dorm on campus. Well, except for the bat problem. But we won't talk about that."

The what?

This is followed by a chorus of "where are you from?" and "what do you like to do?" type questions. I tell them I'm from upstate New York, I was second clarinet in my high school honors band, and I love Russian novels and screwball comedies. I stop there because they already look a little bored. I decide not

11

to bring up my interest in astronomy or the fact that I can recite the periodic table of elements.

Priscilla volunteers that she is from Dallas and wants to go to law school someday. Elinor says that she is from Fair-something, Connecticut, and rides horses. Yoonie adds that she is from Los Angeles and plays the violin. They all seem polite but distant. Of course, I've never been very good at making small talk.

The four of them proceed to discuss their fall schedules: Who's taking French? Who's got Bags for English? Why is there a new photography teacher? Elinor says that Miss Lawrence—the photography teacher?—had to leave because the head-master found out about her affair with Mr. Z.

"Mr. Z? Uh-uh, no way," Priscilla says. "He's, like, old and married . . . and *Asian*." She elbows Yoonie, and the four girls crack up.

"Hey, Asians are tigers in the bedroom," Yoonie says.

"Yeah, I know. Your dad and I hooked up during Parents' Weekend last year," Devon says with a grin.

"Bitch!"

"*Asian* bitch!" Devon snaps back.

They all crack up again.

I have no idea what they're talking about, so I stand there nodding, smiling stupidly, wishing I could make a smooth, graceful exit. But to where? My stomach grumbles. I haven't eaten since breakfast, which was an Egg McMuffin on the Greyhound.

I point to the refreshment table. "Excuse me. I'm just going to . . . um. I'll be right back."

"Ew, that stuff's disgusting, I'd stay away," Elinor says, scrunching up her small, elfin face. "I have Hydroxycut in my purse, do you want one?"

Hydroxycut? "No, I'm good. I'll just . . ." I wave and turn and bump into a chair. The room seems crazy crowded all of a sudden, an obstacle course of furniture and people. I blush and head toward the refreshment table.

"Well, *she's* different," I hear Elinor say behind me.

"Yeah, she's totally not like—" Priscilla's voice drops to a whisper.

I'm totally not like who?

3.

IT'S MY FIRST NIGHT AWAY FROM HOME—AS IN *REALLY* AWAY from home, aside from Girl Scout camp and a few sleepovers and visiting my grandparents' farm in the Finger Lakes. I have a hard time falling asleep; the mattress is too soft, and the sheets Mom bought for me at Target reek of polyester and practically crackle with newness. Plus the radiator hisses and clangs, and the room is insanely *hot*.

I'm not sure where Devon is. It's eleven o'clock, past curfew. I saw her just after dinner, and she said something about a party at a dorm across campus. I lie here, resorting to my usual insomnia trick: counting weeks by Mondays. *Monday, September second; Monday, September ninth; Monday, September sixteenth; Monday, September twenty-third . . .*

Somewhere around November eighteenth, I feel my eyelids grow heavy.

Minutes . . . or hours . . . later, I wake up to the muffled sound of crying. The room is pitch-dark, except for a thin sliver of moonlight slicing through the curtains. Also, the room, which used to be too warm, is now too cold, even though the radiator is still hissing and clanging. Is the window open?

"Devon? Are you okay?" I whisper.

No answer.

I can just make out her form across the room, huddled under her purple silk quilt. For a second I'm unsure what to do. It's not like we're best friends or anything, and she doesn't seem like the crying type, so maybe she just wants to be left alone.

But the sound of her quiet sobbing is so heart-wrenchingly sad that I get up and tiptoe over to her bed. As I pass the window, I check to make sure it's closed. It is.

"Hey, Devon?" I kneel down and tap her shoulder.

She groans and rolls toward me. She smells like sleep and musky perfume. "Hmm? What?"

"Did you have a nightmare, or—"

"Shit, what *time* is it?"

I glance around, totally confused. Devon wasn't crying; the sound was coming from somewhere else in the room, and now it's stopped. "Ohmigosh, I'm so sorry! It's just that I thought you were . . . I mean, I heard someone crying, and I thought it was . . ."

Devon bolts up. Her emerald eyes flash with panic—or maybe the moonlight is playing tricks on me? A second later, they are hard and inscrutable again. "It must be Gita next door. She probably got dumped by her boyfriend. Again," she snipes.

"Oh, okay."

"You interrupted my awesome dream. I was surfing in Bali with two hot locals."

"I'm sorry."

I retreat to my bed, embarrassed. My alarm clock glows 1:49. I shiver and burrow under my comforter.

"Devon?"

"What?"

"Do you think we should go check on her? Gita?"

A heavy sigh. "No, we shouldn't go check on her. I'm sure she'll chill once her Xanax kicks in."

"Oh, okay."

I lie there for a long time listening to Devon toss and turn, wondering why I never get it right, why I'm always making the wrong gesture. I take a deep breath and start to count again: *Monday, September second; Monday, September ninth; Monday, September sixteenth . . .*

⚜ ⚜ ⚜

Devon is talking to someone.

"Please don't be sad. I hate it when you're sad."

Silence.

"No, no, it's not like that!"

Silence.

I blink into the darkness. It's 3:23 a.m. The room is even colder than it was before; my extremities are practically numb.

"Please, let me prove it to you."

Silence.

She must be on the phone. But this late?

The moon is brighter now, and I can see Devon sitting cross-legged on her bed, her body angled away from me.

I can also see her cell charging on her desk.

"Just tell me what to do. You know I always do what you say."

I shift, and one of my pillows bumps up against my nightstand, knocking over an empty Coke can. Devon whirls around. I close my eyes and pretend to be snoring.

Silence and more silence. I can feel Devon's gaze boring into me in the darkness. There's probably a simple explanation for all this: She is talking in her sleep, or drunk, or on drugs, or nuts. Or all of the above. Or maybe I'm having one of those weird dreams that feel completely real. Whatever it is, I wish it would stop.

4.

THE NEXT MORNING, I OVERSLEEP, WHICH I HARDLY EVER DO. I skip my shower and get dressed in two minutes flat, a new record. I don't want to be late for my very first class at Thorn Abbey, an English seminar called The Twentieth-Century Novel.

I see Devon at breakfast, but only for a moment. She is just leaving the Lanyon dining hall as I rush in.

"Sorry if I woke you last night," she apologizes. "I got fucked up at Sophia's party. And then I had this insane nightmare!"

Oh. Mystery solved.

"I was babbling like a crazy homeless person in my sleep, wasn't I? What did I say?" she goes on.

"What? No! Honestly, you didn't bother me at all," I lie.

She gives me one of her dazzling smiles. "Good! Hey, let's

have lunch together later. Meet back here at noon? You don't have any plans, do you?"

"Um, no. Lunch sounds great!"

Actually, I'm incredibly relieved that she invited me. I was worried about having to eat alone in the losers' corner, if this school even has one of those. Or worse yet, taking food back to the room to avoid everyone.

I'm also relieved to know that Devon talks in her sleep sometimes. I never did figure out what was wrong with the heater, but it seemed to be working again by the time I woke up.

Devon and I say good-bye. I grab a poppy seed bagel and scarf down most of it as I head to room 429.

Lanyon seems very old and historical. The hallways are lined with faded photos: class of 1880, class of 1881, and so on and so on. Of course, I manage to get lost. There are so many sets of stairs, some of which go all the way to the top and some of which only go up to a certain floor and then sprout wings and annexes. The place is like a maze.

I finally find room 429. The teacher, Mr. Bagley, is writing some stuff on the blackboard about our summer reading assignment, *The French Lieutenant's Woman.* He peers at me over the top of his tiny, round glasses, then pulls a crumpled index card out of his jacket pocket. "You must be . . . ah, Tess Szekeres. Did I pronounce that right? Have a seat. We were just about to start our discussion."

"I'm so sorry I'm late, I got lost, and—"

"No worries. It's the first day of the new school year."

The room is small and college-like, with a massive oak seminar table and twelve chairs. I take the remaining seat, between a boy with short, coppery hair and a girl I could swear was Mila Kunis. Across from me are two blond girls I recognize from Kerrith. One of them stares pointedly at me, then types something on her iPad and slants it toward the other girl. I cover my mouth, wondering if I have bagel stuck in my teeth.

Mr. Bagley turns from the blackboard and taps one of the words he has written—OUTCAST—with a piece of yellow chalk. "Please elaborate," he says simply. "Anyone? Franklin?"

The boy next to me glances up from his spiral-bound notebook. He and I seem to be the only ones without an iPad or laptop. "Well, the heroine of the book, Sarah Woodruff, is an outcast," he says. "But she brings it on herself. She lies to make herself seem like more of an outsider than she really is."

"Example?" Mr. Bagley prompts him.

"Well, like how she claimed that she'd, uh, had a relationship with a French lieutenant. She hadn't. She just wanted people to think that she was a—"

"Ho," the boy on the other side of Franklin cuts in. Everyone laughs, except for Franklin, who blushes and looks down at his notebook.

Mr. Bagley seems amused. "You're actually onto something, Nate. Even though your choice of vocabulary is rather questionable." He pauses and glances around the room. "So why would Sarah Woodruff want people to think she was a woman of ill repute? Tess?"

Oh, God, Mr. Bagley is calling on me. Does he seriously want me to discuss sex in class? Help!

I clear my throat. "I guess she lied about . . . *that* . . . because in some ways she *wants* to be an outcast. I mean, being an outcast is not fun for her. People judge her and criticize her for being different. But being an outcast also gives her freedom."

"Freedom from?"

"Freedom from Victorian morals and rules. She's completely alone, so she can be her own person and do what she wants."

Mr. Bagley beams. "Yes, yes, that's right, isn't it? Which leads us to our next subject, existentialism."

Okay, that wasn't totally horrible. No one is laughing and pointing at me, although the two Kerrith girls look as though they would if they could. I ignore them and check out the other people sitting around the table. There's Mila Kunis, Franklin, Nate . . .

. . . and then there's this boy at the far end of the table.

He has wavy brown hair and long, slender fingers like a concert pianist. *He's so cute,* is my first thought. Then: *Why is he so sad?* He is staring moodily out the window. At the sea? At something else? I wish I could give him a hug, which is about the dumbest idea ever. I don't even know his name.

Just then, he turns and looks right at me. His dark eyes flash with anger. How utterly humiliating. He thinks I'm spying on him. Which I kind of am. I pick up my pen and pretend to be busy taking notes.

After class is over, I'm the first one out the door. I don't want to run into the two mean Kerrith girls. Or that cute boy, who might accuse me of being a "creeper" the way Jason Delgado did in geometry last year when I *happened* to notice his new haircut. People can be so touchy. Besides, I need to figure out how to get to my Latin class.

But the boy who sat next to me, Franklin, catches me in the hallway as I'm poring over my schedule and campus map. "I think we're the only ones who read the book," he says with a friendly smile. "Do you need help?"

"Room 212M? What does that mean, *M*?"

"*M* stands for 'Mezzanine.' Go down to the first floor, then loop back to the auditorium and take the back stairs up one level."

"Great, thanks."

"By the way, I'm Franklin. Franklin Chase. Are you new here?"

"I'm Tess. I just transferred."

"What do you think of Thorn Abbey so far?"

I hesitate. "It's a lot nicer than my old school," I say, which is the truth. "What about you? How long have you—"

"Franklin!"

That boy, the one who caught me staring, strides over to us. Or rather, to Franklin. He doesn't even acknowledge my existence. "Let's walk to precalc together. I need you to fill me in on what I missed at soccer practice."

"Sure. Tess, this is my roommate, Max. Max, this is Tess. She's new here," Franklin says.

Max's expression is cold and indifferent. Up close, I see that he has a jagged scar on his left cheek. And big shoulders. And beautiful lips.

"Hi!" I hear myself squeak.

"Yeah. Hi. Come on, man, we'll be late," Max says to Franklin.

"Okay, okay. Hey, Tess, do you know about the Monday Night Movie Fest? In Chapin? Maybe we'll see you there tonight," Franklin calls out.

I nod. I have no idea what the Monday Night Movie Fest is.

Max nudges Franklin, and they hurry down the hall. As they turn the corner, Max glances back at me.

Our eyes lock. For a second. Two seconds. An eternity.

Then he is gone.

Why is my heart beating so fast all of a sudden?

5.

"WHAT'S THE MONDAY NIGHT MOVIE FEST?" I ASK DEVON AT lunch, casually.

We are in the Lanyon dining hall, which Devon keeps reminding me is not called a dining hall but the Commons and which looks nothing like the industrial cafetorium at Avery Park High. Everything in the Commons is glossy dark wood, and chandeliers hang from the high, high ceilings.

Devon's phone beeps. She glances at the screen and scowls. "She is *such* an annoying whore."

"Who?"

"My mom. She's constantly texting me with her OCD crap. Why do *I* give a fuck if her Visa's near the credit limit? What were you saying?"

My mom would kill me if I ever called her a whore. I guess Devon doesn't like her mom too much. "The Monday Night Movie Fest. What is it?"

"Oh, that. The Cinema Club runs a movie series every Monday night. It's in the Chapin parlors; Chapin's one of the boys' dorms. What the hell are you eating?"

"It's today's special. Eggplant Parmesan casserole."

"It looks like a miscarriage. And it's going to go straight to your thighs. No offense, but with your body type, you need to be careful about your diet. Otherwise, you're going to end up looking like the Whale." She stabs a cherry tomato with her fork and pops it into her mouth.

Ew. I stop eating and push away my plate. Devon was in such a friendly mood at breakfast. "What whale?"

"Mrs. Hale, the head librarian. We call her Hale the Whale, for obvious reasons. Anyway, I recommend the salad trough. Just avoid the cheese, ham, and croutons. A little white-meat chicken is okay once in a while. Or a hard-boiled egg. But no dressing."

Now I feel fat and humiliated. More humiliated than usual, that is. "So you basically live on lettuce?" I joke feebly.

"This is arugula, not lettuce. Is that what you farm girls from the Midwest call it?"

"I'm not—"

"And yes, I'm very disciplined about what I eat. We all are. But don't worry, I'll get you down to a size zero before you know it."

"Hey, y'all!"

Priscilla makes her way through the Commons and over to our table, along with Elinor and Yoonie. They set their trays down next to ours. Priscilla and Yoonie both have tiny, doll-size salads. Arugula salads. Elinor has a cup of what looks like plain broth.

"I'm still cleansing," Elinor explains. "Day four. One more day to go."

"My grandpa had to do a cleanse last summer. For his colonoscopy," I pipe up.

"I'm sorry. Was I talking to you?" Elinor snaps at me.

My cheeks grow hot. *I shouldn't have opened my mouth. I should never open my mouth.*

Devon turns to Elinor and smacks her on the arm. *Hard.* Elinor's eyes well up with tears. "What the hell?" she cries out.

"Be nice to Tess," Devon says in a steely voice.

"But she was being gross! Who wants to hear about her grandfather's butt operation?" Elinor whines.

"I don't care. She's new here. We should make her feel welcome." Devon turns to Yoonie and Priscilla. "This applies to *all* of you."

"Whatevs," Yoonie says lightly, although she looks a little scared. "I need to stop by the music building. I think I'll skip lunch today."

"I think I'll join you," Elinor says, rubbing her arm. Priscilla gets up too.

The three girls wave and take off.

Devon sighs and shakes her head. "They're not as horrible as they seem. They're super-sweet, once you get to know them."

"O-okay."

I bite my thumbnail, trying to quell my anxiety. At the rate I'm going, I'll never make any friends here. Except Devon, who *has* to speak to me since we're roommates.

I glance around the Commons. No sign of Max. I wonder where he eats lunch, and when. What grade is he in? Do we share any other classes besides English? Mr. Bagley's seminar is only on Mondays, Wednesdays, and Fridays.

Devon reaches over and squeezes my hand. Her nails are painted dark red, almost black. "Listen, I've gotta get my glam on before Spanish. Xander Gates is in my section, can you believe it? I think he's hooking up with Izzy Fallon, but—minor detail. See you back at the convent." She rises to her feet.

I'm pretty sure "the convent" means Kerrith Hall, and I have no idea who Xander Gates or Izzy Fallon are. But I want Devon to like me and don't want to seem any stupider than I already am, so I don't ask. "Right. Oh, and Devon? Do you happen to know . . . I mean, there are so many students here . . . but there's this guy? He's tall with dark brown hair, and I think he plays soccer. His name is Max something," I blurt out.

Devon stops in her tracks and swivels around to face me. "Max De Villiers?" she says slowly. "How do you know him?"

"I don't," I say, surprised by her reaction. "He's in my English class. I just met him this morning, and his roommate Franklin, too."

Devon folds her arms across her chest and is silent for a long moment. What's going on? Do she and Max have some kind of a history?

"He used to date my roommate Becca," Devon says abruptly. "My *ex*-roommate. They were pretty serious."

I wasn't expecting that. "Oh! Did Becca transfer?" I ask hopefully.

"She died."

"She . . . *what?*" I've never known anyone my age who died. Not personally, anyway.

Devon's eyes pool with tears. I feel like a jerk. I just wanted to find out about a cute boy in my class. I had no idea the conversation was going to lead to this.

"I'm so sorry," I say meekly.

"Yeah, well, thanks. It was pretty awful."

"What happened? I mean, how did she . . . ?" I hesitate.

"She drowned. Last spring. The police said that her death was an accident." Devon glances away. "And Max . . . he was totally obsessed with her. He's still not over her, and he probably never will be."

After lunch, I find an empty carrel in the computer center and Google "Becca" and "Thorn Abbey" and "dead." I manage to track down a local newspaper article from May 17, which is less than four months ago. It says that sixteen-year-old Rebecca Rose Winters drowned while sailing in the waters off Whitwater Beach, just down the hill from the school. She was from Philadelphia, the president of the sophomore class, the captain of the girls' tennis team, and a member of the drama club.

She sounds perfect. The opposite of me.

There is no picture with the story. I check out website after website, trying to find one until I run out of time and have to race off to algebra.

I'm not sure why I'm so curious about Becca Winters all of a sudden. I guess it's because Max liked her. And I like Max. My stomach is doing giddy somersaults just thinking about him.

But why? I only met him this morning, and we exchanged like two words. Sure, he's handsome. It's more than that, though. I get the feeling we're similar inside. Different from other people. Outsiders, like the French lieutenant's woman.

I'm not sure how I know all this about him already. I think it was the way he was staring out the window. Or the way we locked eyes as he was walking away. We definitely shared a moment.

Of course, Mom always said that I have a vivid imagination. And I'm a sucker for boys who notice me. It's not something I experience often. Still, maybe if I can learn more about Becca, I can get closer to Max. Find out what kind of girl he likes. And then maybe, just maybe, he'll like me, too?

I'm so pathetic.

6.

A FEW MINUTES BEFORE SEVEN THIRTY, I HURRY INTO THE Chapin parlors and slip into a seat in the back row. Up front, a boy I recognize from Afternoon Assembly is fiddling with a big flat-screen TV. Another boy is operating a popcorn machine, and the air smells like heat and salt and butter. A thirtysomething guy is helping him; I wonder if he's the Mrs. Frith of this dorm?

The room is crowded, but I see Priscilla and Elinor a few rows away, their heads bent close. For a second, I consider joining them. But then I remember what happened at lunch and stay where I am. I can only handle so much rejection in one day.

There is no sign of Max or Franklin. Disappointment washes over me. What did I expect? It was dumb coming here on the slim chance that I might run into Max . . . and on the even slimmer chance that he might want to hang out with me.

I'd been en route to the library, to study. Instead, I walked here as though on autopilot. "I'll only stay for a minute," I murmur, clutching my backpack to my chest. "I'm sure he won't even come." I'm talking to myself just as the two Kerrith girls from my English seminar pass by. They must definitely think I'm a freak now.

"Tess?"

I turn. Franklin is making his way to the seat next to me. My heart skips, and I instinctively glance past him before I even say hi.

And there is Max, looking like he'd rather be in detention or jail. Anywhere but here. Still, my night has just gone from zero to amazing in about two seconds.

"Hey, Franklin. Hey, Max." I give a little wave.

"You made it. That's great!" Franklin nods at the seat on the other side of him. "Max. You promised you'd stay."

"Thanks for the reminder." Max sits down and tries to adjust his long, long legs to fit the cramped space. He glances not so subtly at his watch, which is gold and expensive looking.

"Have you seen it before?" Franklin asks me with a smile.

"Seen what?"

"*To Catch a Thief*. Do you like Alfred Hitchcock?"

"Yes!"

Franklin's smile wavers; he's obviously confused about which question I answered "yes" to. I do like Hitchcock movies, and I've seen this particular film twice. But I don't get a chance to clarify, because the lights dim and the boy up front tells us to enjoy the show. "And try to keep the making out to a minimum, people," he adds with a grin.

I wish.

Franklin shifts in his seat, and his elbow bumps my elbow. "Sorry," he whispers, sounding embarrassed.

"It's okay," I whisper back.

The movie starts, and a woman with cold cream on her face screams about her missing jewels. As the plot unfolds, I'm paying attention but not paying attention, because I'm hyper-aware of Max sitting on the other side of Franklin. If I turn my head slightly and Franklin is leaning back in his seat, I can sort of see Max's rigid, regal profile in the dark.

Is he thinking about Becca? Was he thinking about her in Mr. Bagley's class this morning as he gazed out the window with that lost, lost look?

Or is he maybe, just maybe, thinking about me?

Yeah, dream on.

Someone gives a loud whistle. It's the famous hotel room scene. Grace Kelly is in a strapless white dress and diamonds, and Cary Grant is in a black tux. They flirt like mad until he can't take it anymore and kisses her almost violently. Fireworks explode outside their window as they fall back against the couch.

Max jumps to his feet. "Sorry, homework," he mutters to Franklin, and takes off.

"Maximilian!" Franklin calls after him.

"*Shhhh*," a girl in front of us hisses.

Franklin stares after Max.

"I'll go make sure he's okay," I whisper to Franklin, which is completely random, because what am I doing, offering to check up on Max? He's Franklin's friend, not mine. And it's not like Max said he *wasn't* okay.

But before Franklin can talk me out of it, I get up, grab my backpack, and take off too.

I find Max sitting on a bench in the middle of the quad, tossing pebbles into a massive fountain. Water trickles down from a tall stone pillar that is engraved with the phrase AD PERPETUAM MEMORIAM, which means "in perpetual memory" in Latin. I've been taking Latin since the beginning of freshman year. Most of the other kids at Avery Park chose Spanish or French. Only six of us chose Latin, and I was the least socially challenged in the class. Which is not saying a lot.

I slide onto the bench next to Max. "So I guess you don't like Hitchcock?"

"What? No. He's fine. I just needed to . . ." He pitches a pebble into the water, hard. "It was stuffy in there."

"Yeah, definitely."

He continues flinging pebbles. I know he doesn't want me there, but I can't seem to move. A moment ago, I was on this boy-crush adrenaline high, following him out of the movie. Now I'm frozen with terror. What should I do? What would someone who's *not* socially challenged do?

Probably ask questions, get him to talk about himself.

I clear my throat and clasp my hands in my lap. "Do you live in Chapin?" I ask him politely.

"Yup."

"Do you like it?"

He shrugs. "I've been there since freshman year."

"Are you from around here?"

"New York City. You ask a lot of questions."

Crap. My strategy is backfiring.

"Sorry. I tend to babble when I'm nervous," I admit.

"Why are you nervous?"

"I'm *always* nervous."

He cracks a smile.

"I'm from Avery Park," I volunteer. "I'm sure you've never heard of it. It's this incredibly depressing suburb upstate."

"Why do you live there if it's so depressing?"

"I'm not sure. We've always lived there. My mom works as a receptionist at the chip plant."

"Like potato chips?"

"If only. Semiconductor chips. A potato chip plant would have been way better, though. Free samples. I'm a huge sour cream and onion fan."

Max cracks another smile. I will myself to shut up. He's used to sophisticated, salad-eating Thorn Abbey girls like Devon. And Becca.

I start to bite my nails, then stop. A minute passes, then two. A few students walk across the quad, going in and out of the library. But other than that, things are totally dead, including my non-conversation with Max.

He looks up at the sky. I look up too. It's velvet black and dotted with stars. I try to make out the Big Dipper, Orion, the Pleiades.

"If we had to do it all over again, do you think we'd see the same constellations that people saw thousands of years ago?" I muse. "I mean, maybe we wouldn't see a big dipping thing or a hunter's belt or whatever. Maybe we'd see completely different patterns. It's all a matter of perspective, right?"

Max picks up another pebble and aims it at the pillar. He hits it with a loud thunk. "You're kind of strange. You know that, right?" he says after a moment.

I blush furiously. *He* thinks I'm a freak too.

"Besides, the Big Dipper and Orion's Belt aren't constellations. They're asterisms." He stands up. "I've gotta go. See you in Bags's class. Thanks." He smiles, turns, and walks away.

Hope flutters in my chest.

He smiled at me. For real. And he thanked me for . . . well, I'm not sure what, but *something*. Was he flirting with me just now? Maybe he doesn't hate me after all.

Back at Kerrith Hall, I check in with the security guard in the lobby and race up the stairs, two at a time. My thoughts are in a mad, happy jumble. Max. Maximilian. Maximilian De Villiers.

Tonight felt like a breakthrough. Max and I made a connection. A tiny, fledgling connection, but still. I'm sure it hasn't been easy for him to find the right person to help him move on after Becca's death. After all, we deep, smart, solitary types have a tough time relating to people who aren't like us.

But now Max has me. As a friend. Even as more than a friend. Whatever he wants.

I haven't had a crush on a boy in ages, not since Will Weikart in eighth grade. Will and I were in band together. One day during rehearsal, he gave me this *look*. Kind of like the one Max gave me this morning after class. No boy had ever looked at me that way before, as if I were cute or interesting or special, and in that instant, I decided that Will and I should become boyfriend-girlfriend. Which never quite happened. He kissed me once, in the parking lot after the holiday concert while I was standing in the freezing cold with my clarinet case, waiting for my mom to pick me up. That was the extent of our relationship. After the holiday break, he acted like he had no idea who I was. I texted him a bunch of times, but he never texted back.

Maybe things will be different with Max.

When I reach the second-floor landing, I hear the faint strains of pop music, voices, laughter. There is no one in the halls, though, and everyone's door is closed. I wonder if Devon is still up. I wonder if I can get her to tell me about Max and Becca's relationship. The more I know about the two of them, the easier it will be to get closer to Max.

I am almost at the third-floor landing when someone taps my shoulder. I whirl around, surprised.

As I turn, my feet go out from under me with a sudden, swift force. I fall, and my face slams hard against the wooden step. I cry out in pain and touch the raw, tender place on my cheek. I can already feel a bruise forming.

"You shouldn't sneak up on people!" I shout at whoever was behind me.

But no one is there.

7.

"*OW! THAT HURTS!*"

"Oh, shut it," Devon orders me. She holds my head still with one hand while she rubs a weird-smelling cream on my face. "I know it stings, but it's good for you."

"What is it, anyway?"

"It's a special blend. My acupuncturist made it for me when I messed up my leg at Killington."

"What's Killington?"

"Really, Tess? It's a ski resort in Vermont."

Noted. I add "Killington" to my mental Thorn Abbey cultural literacy checklist. I have to stop being so clueless if I'm ever going to fit in. I wonder if Max skis? Does he go to this Killington place too?

Devon leans back and scrutinizes her handiwork. "God, you look like a poster child for domestic violence. Are you sure you didn't get into a girl fight?"

"I told you, I tripped on the stairs. I thought someone was following me, and—"

"Yeah, yeah, yeah. You've got to stop being such a klutz. These buildings are older than dirt, and don't even get me started on the fire hazards. Elinor and I were smoking in the third-floor lounge one night, and we almost burned the place down. The walls are, like, made of straw."

"You're allowed to smoke cigarettes here?" I ask, surprised.

"Seriously? No, you're not allowed to smoke anywhere on campus. Besides, I wasn't talking about cigarettes." Devon sighs. "Stay there. I'm just going to put a piece of gauze on that so the cream stays on while you sleep."

"Okay, thanks."

She twists her shiny black hair up in a clip and pads over to the closet in her fuzzy slippers. She looks like a Victoria's Secret model in her flannel pajama bottoms and multiple tank tops. When I wear stuff like that, I just look sloppy, like it's laundry day.

Clothes rustle, stuff falls, Devon swears, and a minute later, she returns with a giant first-aid kit. "My mom made me bring it. She's a doctor," she explains.

"Really? What kind of doctor?"

"A cardiologist."

"Wow, she must be smart."

"She's a psychotic bitch."

"Oh."

I wonder what Devon means by that. Is her mom really crazy and mean, or does Devon just not get along with her? Should I ask Devon, or would she be offended? I'm not used to having intimate conversations with other girls. Or boys. Or anyone, for that matter.

Devon takes a square of gauze and lays it gently across my face. It feels light, almost imperceptible, like butterfly wings. I close my eyes and try to figure out what happened on the stairs. Maybe Devon's right. Maybe I'm just a klutz. But I could have sworn someone tapped me on the shoulder. Was I so busy daydreaming about Max that I imagined the whole thing?

"I just need to tape this up, and you'll be all set," Devon says.

"This is really sweet of you, thanks."

"What are roommates for, right?" She rips off a piece of surgical tape. "So where were you tonight, anyway?"

I blink. "I went to that Monday night movie thing."

"You did? Who'd you go with?" she asks skeptically.

"I went, you know, by myself."

Devon smirks. I must sound pretty pathetic. "I saw Elinor and Priscilla there," I name-drop hastily.

"Did you sit with them?"

Okay, so how do I answer that? I don't want to admit that I was too scared to ask Elinor and Priscilla if I could join them. That would *definitely* make me sound pathetic. On the other hand, I don't want to mention Max. Devon's friend's ex-boyfriend. But if I *don't* mention him, she might find out anyway.

"No. I would have, but that Franklin guy showed up. The one from my English seminar? And he was with his—with Max De what's-his-name. They sat down next to me," I blurt out finally.

Devon stares at me.

"I didn't really speak to them, because the movie started," I say in a rush. "*To Catch a Thief.* It's amazing. Did you ever see it?"

She doesn't answer. I realize that the "not talking to them" part isn't exactly true. And she probably didn't buy how I mangled Max's name.

But I've told her enough. I seriously don't want her to know that I stalked Max out of Chapin and that we *did* talk. A lot. I think Devon's starting to warm up to me. If she figures out that I'm interested in Max, she'll probably hate me forever out of loyalty to Becca or whatever.

"She loved that movie," Devon says quietly.

"I'm sorry. Who?"

"Becca. *To Catch a Thief* was one of her favorites. Have I

---

always, forever

shown you a picture of her? She looks like Grace Kelly, actually."

Grace Kelly? "Um, no."

Devon walks over to her dresser and rummages through a small wooden chest, dumping out earrings, bracelets, strands of pearls. Finally, she plucks out a tiny silver key. Then she sits down at her desk, opens the bottom drawer, and pulls out a box. It's large and flat and silver and etched with some sort of flower design.

She opens the box with the key and touches whatever's inside gingerly, the way she touched the gauze on my cheek. The box seems special and romantic, like the sort of box I would keep love letters in. If anybody ever wrote me love letters, that is.

She pulls out a photograph and brings it over to me. "Here. That's her."

I hesitate for a second before taking the photo from Devon. Earlier, I was anxious to see what Becca looked like. But now I'm not so sure.

"Isn't she pretty?" Devon prompts me. "Grace Kelly, right?"

I force myself to look. A tall, slim girl poses in front of a sailboat, smiling and waving at the camera. She's wearing a tiny white bikini, and her pale blond hair is blowing in the wind.

My chest tightens. Becca isn't just pretty. She's radiantly, gloriously beautiful. Grace Kelly beautiful. And she has this air of innocent sweetness that makes you not want to hate her for it.

But at the moment, I do. Hate her. Because how can I compete with that? She is obviously perfect inside *and* out.

Was, I mean.

"We were all so worried about Max after she died," Devon says, gazing wistfully at the photo. "He kind of stopped living. Like he had no reason to go on. He still seems that way, doesn't he? But I guess you don't know him that well."

I gnaw on my thumbnail. I thought Max was starting to warm up to me. Like Devon. So much for that.

"You should stay away from him. Becca and I used to be roommates; now *you're* my roommate, and you'd just remind him of her. You know what I mean?"

I don't answer. This conversation makes me want to cry.

"Tess? Are you listening to me?"

"Y-yes. I heard you."

Devon smiles and kisses the top of my head. "Good girl. How's your cheek? Does it still hurt? You should take a couple of Advil or Tylenol before you go to sleep. And if that doesn't do the trick, I've got some stuff that'll really take the pain away."

I think about Max, about how quickly our non-relationship bloomed and then died. Is this what a broken heart feels like? I doubt there are any pills for that. Besides, I have no right to a broken heart. I never had a chance to get that far with Max.

I can't sleep.

For a while I lie staring at the ceiling, counting Mondays. Around two a.m. I switch to Tuesdays, then to Wednesdays, but that doesn't work either. I eventually give up and drink warm Coke and read some American history chapters with my penlight.

Around four a.m., I decide to get up and go for a walk. I can't stand being in the room anymore. I put on a hoodie over my pajamas and pull on my fake Uggs over my SpongeBob socks. I grab my keys and slip out the door, careful not to wake Devon, who is crazy-talking in her sleep again. Something about a dress.

The halls of Kerrith are deathly quiet. I'm extra careful going down the stairs, holding the railing the whole way. In the lobby, the security guard isn't at his post. It's too late, or early, even for him.

Outside, I breathe in the chilly, foggy air. It's only September, but it's super-cold. The grass under my feet is soft with dew. The sky is dark, moonless, and overcast. There is no Big Dipper, no Orion's Belt—no constellations or asterisms or stars whatsoever.

And then, for some reason I can't quite explain, I begin walking toward the beach. Whitwater Beach. I quickly cross the deserted quad, passing the fountain with the stone pillar. At the edge of the woods, I find the trailhead that Devon pointed out when she was showing me around on Sunday.

I hurry along the narrow dirt path, crossing my arms over my chest to try to get warm, and it occurs to me that maybe this isn't the smartest idea: hiking down to the beach, alone, in the dark. In my pajamas. I didn't even leave a note telling Devon where I was going or think to bring a flashlight or my phone.

Still, I don't stop and go back. Something drives me onward. *It's where she died*, I tell myself. *It's the last place where she was alive.* But why do I care about Becca Winters? Is it because I have a stupid, hopeless crush on her ex-boyfriend?

I feel so dumb, like I'm in eighth grade again, pining over Will Weikart. When he didn't return my texts, I went over to my friend Kayleigh's house and we polished off an entire half gallon of Philly Vanilla ice cream plus a bag of potato chips. The next day I had the worst stomachache, along with a gigantic new zit on my forehead. And at lunch, Will was making out with that slutty Danielle Gump in the cafetorium.

My love life definitely sucks. Then, now, forever.

When I reach the crest of the path, I can make out a sliver of ocean. I have to figure out how to get down to the water. I haven't been to the beach—any beach—in ages, not since my mom and I drove to Cape Cod when I was in third grade. We were visiting her friend Noreen, who worked at a motel there and got us a room for cheap. I remember the massive waves on the Atlantic and the screaming, happy kids on their boogie boards . . . and the calmer waters of the bay with toddlers splashing in tide pools and couples reading the Sunday paper. I remember peachy sunsets and eating fried clams and soft serve with my mom while we strolled around the pier, checking out the fancy yachts. She would talk about the big boats with a mixture of pleasure and envy that I didn't understand back then.

But these woods, this path, and the beach beyond bear little resemblance to Cape Cod. Everything about this place is cold and uninviting. Of course, it's probably the early hour of the day and my foul mood. Or the fact that a girl I didn't even know, a girl who's been on my mind way too much since yesterday, drowned in these waters.

I stop in my tracks. There's no good reason for me to be here. I have zero business chasing ghosts or chasing Max De Villiers, which is basically what I'm doing. I'm tired and freezing, and I'd be better off back in Kerrith Hall with a cup of vending-machine hot chocolate and my comforter.

That's when I see him. He is standing on a rocky cliff, holding a bottle in his hand, his feet precariously close to the edge.

Oh my God, he's going to jump.

"Max! *No!*" I scream.

8.

MAX DOESN'T TURN. I BREAK INTO A RUN, SHOUTING HIS NAME.

"Max! *Don't!*"

He flings the bottle toward the sea, yelling something. It sounds like "die," but it's hard to hear over the wind and the waves crashing below. Plus my heart is pounding, practically bursting out of my chest. I won't get to him in time.

He wants to be with Becca.

I force myself to run faster, faster—and somehow, by some miracle, I manage to reach him before he goes over. I'm so freaked out I can barely think. I grab fistfuls of his navy school sweater and try to yank him back from the ledge. But he's way bigger than I am, and he barely budges. He doesn't even seem to notice I'm there.

I catch sight of the precipice below: a sheer cliff wall ending in a churning black abyss. My stomach twists. I'm afraid of heights. And here I am, teetering on the edge of the world with a suicidal boy, and we're *both* going to die.

I burst into tears, still clutching Max's sweater. I've never been so terrified. He finally regards me with a blank look. His eyes are red, as if he's been crying too. He doesn't seem to know who I am.

"Max, it's *me*!" I sob.

Still nothing. It's like he's in a trance.

"Please, please! You don't want to die. *I* don't want to die. You need to step away from there, okay? Here, take my hand."

He blinks and slips his hand into mine, and I coax him back from the ledge. He's obviously wasted; he reeks of whiskey. Alcohol and grief—great combination.

Once we're on safer ground, away from the cliff, I lead him toward the woods with quicker steps. Just then, a gray seagull swoops by, so close that I flinch. It circles us once and flies away, its screech falling on us like broken glass.

For a split second, the seagull glows bright white against the predawn sky. But the sun isn't up yet. I must be hallucinating. Max frowns at the bird but says nothing.

We reach the trail leading back to campus. I let go of Max's hand and lean against a tree to catch my breath. Off to the side of the path is a sign that I didn't notice before: DANGER: NO HIK-ING BEYOND THIS POINT. Somewhere in the woods, I must have taken a wrong turn. And yet it led me to Max.

I swipe at my tears with my sleeve. "What the fuck?" I say finally.

Max's gaze flicks toward me.

"Seriously, what the fuck?" I repeat, raising my voice. I've never spoken to anyone like that before, but now that I've started, I can't stop. "I know we don't know each other very well, but honestly, what were you *thinking?*"

Max closes his eyes and rubs his temples. Maybe I'm getting through to him.

"Are you completely selfish?" I continue. "Do you want to destroy the lives of everyone who's ever cared about you? Is that what *she* would have wanted? Becca?"

Her name escapes my lips before I can stop myself. I didn't mean to say it. Devon warned me not to upset him.

Now he is completely alert. He glares at me, squeezing his fists as though he wants to punch something. "*What* did you say?"

I step back out of his reach. I don't think he'd hit me, but you never know with a drunk person. "I—I'm sorry she's gone. "I really, really am. But she's not worth dying for. No one is."

His expression darkens. He looks tormented. "You don't know what you're talking about," he whispers hoarsely.

"Yes, I do! This boy from my old school, Paulie, jumped off a bridge last winter because he found out his girlfriend was cheating on him. He's still in a coma."

Max shakes his head and starts down the path. "Please. Just leave me alone."

"No! You need help!" I plant myself in front of him.

But he's moving too fast and I stumble backward, hitting the ground. "*Ow!*"

Suddenly Max is kneeling beside me, flustered, full of apologies. "I'm sorry! Are you all right? Did I hurt you?"

I do a quick mental scan. "I'm fine," I mutter angrily.

"Here, take my hand."

He carefully lifts me to my feet. For a moment, we're standing so close that our bodies are practically touching. I was so furious with him a moment ago. Now all I can think about is how beautiful and sad his eyes are and how warm his hand feels in mine.

My friend Kayleigh always told me that I should learn to "seize the day." Is this one of those days? Should I just forget about what almost happened on the cliff and give in to the here and now? If I pretend to be dizzy, I could swoon against Max's big, strong chest and he could press his mouth against my hair and—

"Are you all right?" he repeats.

I nod mutely. I don't trust myself to speak.

"Wait, did I do that?" He touches the bandage on my cheek.

I laugh. "I had a little accident earlier. On the stairs, in my dorm."

"Oh." He sounds relieved. "Do you do that often?"

"No. You really *are* drunk, aren't you?"

"Maybe a little."

"Do you do that often?"

He hesitates and looks away. "It was a bad night."

"Do you want to talk about it?" I ask him gently.

"Not at the moment, no."

I bite my lip. I wish he would confide in me. I want so much to comfort him and take his sadness away.

Or do I want more than that? To be honest, I still like him. *Really* like him. Even though he's so not over Becca that he almost jumped off a cliff.

What is wrong with me?

He runs his hand through his hair, making it stick this way and that. Even rumpled and wasted and in the throes of whatever madness he is experiencing, Max is incredibly handsome. I, on the other hand, must look ridiculous in my mud-splattered pajamas.

We stand there for a while, staring out at the predawn sky, which has morphed into a bruise-like palette of purples and yellows. Herons, egrets, and other large, primeval-looking birds arc through the air. I feel as though we are the only people on the planet. Max's breathing quiets, and I instinctively match the rhythm of my breath with his. The moment is so surreal, and, in its own way, perfect.

He gazes into my eyes and leans in until his face is just inches away from mine.

Oh my God. He's going to kiss me. . . .

"We should get back," he says abruptly.

. . . *or not.* I turn away, trying to hide my disappointment. "Do you want me to take you to the school nurse? Or call your parents?" I ask him.

"I'm fine. Really. But thanks for your concern." He glances at my hoodie and pajamas. "You must be freezing."

"A little."

"Come on."

He drapes his arm around me, and we start down the wooded path toward campus. Giant tree branches lace over our heads like a cathedral ceiling. Okay, so he didn't kiss me. But he *is* sort of holding me in a romantic way.

Even though he probably won't remember any of this later, when he's sober.

Even though I know now, with one hundred percent certainty, that I never had a chance with him.

It's just as well, right?

9.

I'm not sure how I got through the morning. First I had to sneak back into my room without waking Devon, who would have asked a million nosy questions. Fortunately, she was out cold, not even crazy-talking in her sleep.

Then I took an extra-long shower, got dressed in my school uniform, downed two cups of vending-machine hot chocolate, and checked over my homework twice. At that point, I was running on pure adrenaline. But by the time I got to my first-period class, Intro to Philosophy, I started to crash. By Latin, I could barely keep my eyes open, especially during verb conjugations. I got *amat* mixed up with *amant*, and the teacher made some joke about it that I totally didn't understand. By American history and the founding fathers, I was practically vegetative.

Now it's lunchtime, and instead of eating and socializing, I'm in the computer center. I really should be taking a quick nap, but I wanted to see if maybe, just maybe, Max has sent me an e-mail. I figured that since it's Tuesday, and we didn't have English together this morning, he may have wanted to thank me for saving his life or whatever.

My in-box contains exactly three messages, and none of them are from him. Oh well.

Of course, I could always write him first, and then he would feel obligated to write back:

Dear Max,

Just wanted to say hi!

Hope you're feeling better!

Tess

PS Do you believe in love at first sight?

Delete, delete, delete.

Sigh. I seized the day, and I failed. Kayleigh thinks that "seize the day" is a line from her favorite pop song. I've told her it's actually a translation of *carpe diem*, from a poem by Horace. Which makes me the smart, nerdy girl who knows two-thousand-year-old Latin poetry. Not that it's going to get me kissed by Max anytime soon. Or ever.

I read my e-mail. The first is from the Dean of Students, regarding upcoming events. There is a boys' soccer game on Saturday. I jot down the details on a piece of scrap paper. It might be my only chance to "accidentally" run into Max this weekend. So far, we only seem to share the one class, English. Which means I may have to be more creative. *Give it up*, I tell myself sternly. I crumple the paper and toss it in the trash.

The second e-mail is from my mom:

Honey bunny!

I hope you are doing well and settling in at Thorn Abbey. The house seems so empty without you, just me and Marshmallow Fluff, who sleeps with me now that you're not around.

How do you like your classes? Did you decide to take sculpture or painting for your art elective? What is your dorm like? Are you making lots of new friends? Please write and tell me everything ASAP!

Do you need me to mail you anything from home? Let me know. I can run over to the Pack 'n' Ship during my lunch hour.

Love you forever,

Mom

I get a little teary-eyed, reading her e-mail. I'm so used to seeing her every day, puttering around the house doing Mom stuff. It's Tuesday, so if I were home, she'd be making tacos for dinner. Friday we'd watch back-to-back episodes of *Law & Order*, the two of us competing to see who could solve the mystery first. Sundays are always Swedish pancakes for breakfast. And so on and so on. Mom is into family rituals. She calls them "mental vitamins."

I write her a detailed reply, signing off with lots of *x*'s and *o*'s, before I open the third e-mail, from Kayleigh. Kayleigh was my closest friend in Avery Park, sort of, because she lives down the street and we were both in band and she didn't think I was a freak for being a straight-A student. She's pretty much the only reason I didn't have to sit in the losers' corner of the cafetorium. But lately, she's become obsessed with witches and unicorns and other supernatural stuff that I can't quite relate to. Her parents are getting divorced, so I guess she has an excuse.

Hey, Girl!! ☺

How are you doing in your fancy rich kid school? I bet everyone there is a genius like you haha.

Guess what happened?! And I swear I'm not making this up. Last nite these three angels visited me in my dreams! They told me that Paulie Wozniak is going to wake up soon and that he's going to be OK!

I'm not sure if I should tell Paulie's mom and dad about

this or what. PRO: They deserve to know, right? CON: It might be weird cuz they never talk about Paulie anymore. I know cuz whenever I babysit his sister Corey, they act all fake cheerful like everything's fine and not like their son is lying in St. Michael's in a coma. What do you think I should do???

ANYWAY, not much else going on here. School is super-boring as always. Pretty much the entire football team was arrested for smoking pot at Kyle Oestreicher's house Saturday nite, and now they're talking about canceling the Homecoming game. BIG YAWN. Oh, and the parental units are still insane and fighting over the family fortune haha. I CANNOT WAIT for one of them to move out. I'm secretly hoping it's Mom. Remember that time she had to go to Detroit on a "business trip" and you slept over and Dad let us eat Dove Bars for dinner? Life could be phenom for us with him in charge. ☺

Well, except you're not here. I miss you! But maybe I could visit you some weekend? I checked out the website and Thane Abby looks GORGEOUS from the pix. Plus the boys look daaamn fine. ☺

Wait, pictures? Of the students?

I quickly switch over to the Thorn Abbey home page and locate a link in the corner that says GALLERY. I don't remember seeing this when Mom and I were researching private schools last winter. Of course, I wasn't really thinking about daaamn fine boys, either.

I click and begin scrolling. Images blur by: random kids in class, in the Lanyon Commons, at a dance. There is Yoonie, playing the violin. There is Franklin, peering through a microscope. There is what's-his-name, Nate, from Mr. Bagley's class, kicking a soccer ball. I keep scrolling, looking for Becca or Max. But there is nothing.

And then, at the bottom of a page, there it is: a picture of the two of them walking through a snow-covered quad. Becca is wearing a cream-colored coat, leggings, and boots. Max is wearing a leather jacket and jeans. Her hand is tucked cozily in his pocket, and he is smiling down at her. His happy, relaxed expression seems completely at odds with the Max I know.

I lean into the screen, squinting, frowning. They look perfect together. There's no other way to describe it. She is so beautiful, and he is so beautiful, and they are so obviously and madly in love.

"Tess?"

I startle. Franklin has materialized at my side. I try to gracefully block the screen so he can't see that I'm cyber-stalking his roommate. "Franklin! Hi!"

"I'm so glad I ran into you. Have you eaten yet? Do you

want to grab some lunch?" As always, he is the epitome of friendly.

"Actually, I have to . . ." I'm so rattled, not to mention sleep deprived, that I can't even come up with a suitable lie. I glance around the computer center, which is pretty much empty except for a couple of guys printing documents and talking loudly: "And then she walks in on me getting with her roommate, and I'm like, 'What's your problem,' and she's like . . ."

"Actually, I already ate. But I'll walk with you?" I say to Franklin.

"Sure. Hey, what did you do to your face?"

"Oh, you know, big klutz. It looks worse than it is."

He raises his eyebrows. "Wow. I'm glad you're okay."

I close out of my computer account, double-checking to make sure I'm really and truly signed out, and we head off together. We pass a girl leaving the ladies' room, tucking a tube of pink lip gloss into her backpack. Not that she needs it. Is physical attractiveness a prerequisite for getting into Thorn Abbey, and if so, why did they let me in? I'm sure they'll never include *my* picture on their website. *We need to work on that self-esteem of yours, honey bunny*, I can hear my mom saying.

I think I have a tube of lip gloss somewhere. Kayleigh made me buy it at CVS over the summer. Maybe I should start using it.

"So you missed the best part of the movie," Franklin says.

"What?"

"Last night? *To Catch a Thief?*"

"Oh, right! Actually, I know how it ends. I've seen it before."

"You have? Me too. Three or four times. I have a crush on Grace Kelly, along with every other guy on this planet." Franklin grins. "Well, every other guy on this planet who likes old movies."

Have I shown you a picture of her? She looks like Grace Kelly, actually.

"Tess?"

"Hmm?"

Franklin touches my arm. "Are you okay?"

I force a smile. I'm so not in the mood to be reminded about how amazing Becca was. "I'm fine. Just trying to remember if I finished my algebra homework."

"Really? You don't seem like the not-finishing-homework type," he jokes.

"Well, there's always a first time, right?" I joke back.

"Right. Hey, I meant to ask you." Franklin lowers his voice. "Did you ever find Max after he went flying out of Chapin? He can be a little intense."

I hesitate. Franklin must not have heard about the cliff incident this morning.

"I know about Becca," I confess.

He stares at me. "You do?"

"I heard about it from—from some people, and it's awful! I can't imagine what Max must be going through. No wonder he's, um, intense, like you said." I'm speaking very fast, and I probably sound a little nuts. But I'm dying to talk to someone, anyone, about Max and Becca, especially after what almost happened this morning.

The *two* things that almost happened this morning.

"Were you friends with her, too?" I rush on, noticing Franklin's silence. "How long did she and Max go out? Was he the one who found her body, or—"

"Tess," Franklin interrupts, and this time his voice is not friendly. "You've got the wrong idea about Max. He's my best friend. We grew up together, and I probably know him better than anyone. He's not who he appears to be. He's got issues, and it's probably best if you steer clear of him."

10.

It's Wednesday morning, and I have downsized the bandage on my cheek so I don't look as banged up as I did before. Of course, this doesn't keep the two Kerrith girls from shooting me judgmental looks in Mr. Bagley's class.

Unfortunately, Max is not looking at me at all, judgmentally or otherwise. He is sitting in the same seat as Monday, his gaze fixed on his laptop screen. I keep trying to catch his attention, but it's as if I don't exist. Although, to be fair, he seems to be ignoring everyone—not just me.

Why is this happening? I haven't seen him or heard from him since the drama yesterday on the cliff. I actually spent time getting ready this morning—brushing my unruly hair, applying lip gloss—because I knew he'd be here.

Except, he's *not* here. He's somewhere else. Again.

I force myself to snap out of my Max trance and pay attention to Mr. Bagley. "For those of you who actually finished the novel, you were no doubt surprised by the fact that it has two endings. In the first ending, Charles Smithson and Sarah Woodruff live happily ever after. In the second ending, Charles and Sarah part ways. Why did John Fowles write it this way?" he asks the class.

Franklin sits next to Max, which is completely awkward, because every time I glance in Max's direction, Franklin's alert eyes flash with warning. Why did he tell me to steer clear of Max? For that matter, why did Devon? In her case, I guess she's worried that I will remind Max of Becca because I'm the new roommate, which will make him seriously depressed. But Franklin made it seem like I should be careful for my own sake.

Why? What sorts of "issues" does Max have—besides mourning his dead girlfriend, that is? He and I definitely have a connection. I felt it when we first met, at the fountain, and even on the cliff. Most of all on the cliff. He was *this close* to kissing me. I could so help him move on, if only he would let me.

The Kerrith girls are still gawking at me. I cover my bandaged cheek with my hand and lean into it, like I'm contemplating deep thoughts. I don't think they're buying it, though, and besides, the pressure makes the pain worse.

"Tess?"

I bolt up in my seat. Mr. Bagley smiles patiently at me.

"Yes?"

"Any insights? On John Fowles's dual ending?"

"Oh! I think it has to do with his philosophy of existentialism. Fowles didn't believe that there was one absolute truth or reality. He believed that people are free, that they have choices. So he gave his two main characters the freedom to choose their own destinies."

"Very good, Tess! Does anyone else have anything to add?"

The French Lieutenant's Woman is insanely romantic. I loved the ending where Charles and Sarah are reunited after a long separation and he finds out that she had his baby in secret and they realize that they belong together.

Of course, I hated the alternate ending, where Charles and Sarah can't make it work and he moves to another continent forever. Why can't all love stories end happily?

I glance across the table at Max. He's still staring pensively at his laptop. I have no idea what he's thinking or feeling right now. *Ugh.* Obviously, I understand fictional characters better than real people. At least I'll get an A in this class, even if I get an F in Max 101.

Mr. Bagley announces that we have to come up with a paper topic plus a short outline by Friday. I add this to my to-do list, which is already looking pretty long. There's definitely a lot of homework in private school.

At nine forty-five, when class is over, Max practically speed-walks out the door. Not even a "hi" or a "bye" or a "thank you for pulling me back from the edge of the cliff"? I gather my stuff, my mood suddenly as gray as the sky outside. The two Kerrith girls and Mila Kunis are gabbing about their hot dates with their hot boyfriends on Friday night, which makes me feel even worse.

"Hi, Tess!" Franklin pauses by my chair on his way out.

"What?" I snap.

He laughs. "Was it something I said?"

"I'm sorry. It's just this headache," I improvise. Why am I being so rude to Franklin? I'm not usually a rude person, and besides, he's been nothing but nice to me since I got here.

I'd better start over. "Soooo. How are you? How's life?"

"Life is excellent. Are you on your way to Latin?"

"Yes. What about you?"

"Precalc. Mr. Millstein. You're a sophomore, right? You'll get him next year."

We head into the hallway, and I listen politely as Franklin goes on about Mr. Millstein's infamous pop quizzes. But I can't stop thinking about what he said about Max. Maybe I should just ask him what he meant, point-blank.

But before I can open my mouth, I spot Max in the crowded hallway, leaning against a trophy case filled with medals. When he sees me, he straightens and shoots me a shy half smile. "Hi, Tess."

"Max!"

I mumble "Excuse me" to Franklin and hurry to Max's side. "Hi! Are you okay? I mean, how are you?" I babble.

"I'm good, thanks. Listen, are you doing anything tonight?"

Confused, I glance over my shoulder. Is Max talking to me? *Oh my God, he's talking to me.* I notice Franklin hanging back and checking his phone.

"Tess?" Max prompts me.

"What? Yes! I thought—" I take a deep breath so as to stop sounding like a complete idiot. "Let's see, tonight? I had this thing, but I don't have it anymore. Yeah, I'm definitely free."

"I thought maybe we could meet at the library and work on those paper topics for Bags."

"Sure!"

"Say, at eight? If you give me your number, I can text you."

"Sure!"

I try to sound calm, cool, and collected, like his invitation is no big deal. But it's hard to keep from jumping up and down and screaming with joy.

We exchange numbers. From zero attention to a study date.

I wonder what changed? But maybe that's just how boys act. It's not like I have a lot of experience in that department. Grinning, I type his name into my contact list as MAX!!! with three exclamation points.

"What's so funny?" he asks me.

"What? Oh, I was just thinking about how much smaller cell phones will get in the future," I reply, attempting to cover up my dumb crush behavior. Pretty soon, I'll be scribbling "I ♥ MAX" in my notebook with glittery pink markers.

He shakes his head with a smile. "Yeah, you're definitely strange."

"Uh, thanks?"

He waves and takes off. Franklin is waiting for him a little ways down the crowded hall. He tucks his phone in his pocket and says something to Max.

As they walk away, Franklin turns and gives me that warning look. I know what he's thinking. But I don't care.

I head down the hall in the other direction, practically skipping.

I have a date with Max.

I have a date with Max.

I have a date with Max.

11.

AT LUNCH, I EAT A BIG PLATE OF DRESSINGLESS, TASTELESS RAW vegetables while Devon tells Priscilla, Elinor, Yoonie, and me about the improvements she wants to make to the Kerrith third-floor lounge. I bite into a carrot stick and take a big sip of water—room temperature, with a slice of lemon, the way Devon told me to drink it—and feel myself getting skinnier and prettier. And hungrier. How do these people survive on so little food? And just how skinny and pretty will I get by eight o'clock, when I meet up with Max?

"We could get a new DVD player plus some new furniture. And maybe an Xbox, too," Devon says. "The stuff we have now is basically flea market crap. I thought it would be nice to make some changes, start the year fresh." She shrugs and smiles sadly.

"Oh, sweetie." Priscilla reaches across the table and squeezes Devon's hand. "I think that's an *awesome* idea."

"We are totally with you on this," Elinor adds.

"Big-time." Yoonie gives two thumbs-up.

I wonder what Devon and the girls are talking about. Do they mean "start the year fresh" because of what happened to Becca? I wish I could jump into their discussion, but I don't want to intrude or say the wrong thing. Especially not after my idiotic colonoscopy remark the other day.

"So I talked to Mrs. Frith, and she says we can redecorate if we pay for it ourselves." Devon continues, "Does anyone have any ideas? Priscilla, your parents will pitch in, right?"

"Hit up the Texas oil tycoons," Priscilla jokes. "Seriously, they'll totally send me a check. They never ask questions. What about your mom and dad, Devon? They're loaded, too, right?"

"I texted my mom about it this morning. She said she has to think about it. Her divorce lawyer is charging her a fortune and she has to be careful with her money or whatever. Of course, if she wasn't such a selfish bitch, there wouldn't be a divorce to begin with." Devon sighs. "I guess I can try my dad, though. I can usually guilt him into letting me use his AmEx card."

I stare at Devon. I had no idea her parents were splitting up.

"Mother and Dad will send me a check if I ask. I'll tell them I need to replace my Burberry. They'll never notice," Elinor volunteers.

"I'll tell mine I need a new bow for my violin," Yoonie adds.

"Perfect." Devon turns to me. "Tess, what about you?"

"I guess I can ask my mom," I say reluctantly. My mom can barely afford rent and groceries, much less fancy furniture and DVD players and Xboxes for our dorm. But I don't want to tell the girls that.

"What about your dad? Are they divorced?" Devon asks.

I hesitate. I really don't want to get into my depressing family history. "Sort of," I say vaguely.

"Sort of? You're quite the mystery, aren't you? I'm going to have to Google you, Tess. I bet you're like the crown princess of some no-name country, and the bad haircut and discount shoes are all an act to fit in with us lowly mortals."

I feel the blood drain from my face. Does Devon know that I've been cyber-stalking Becca? I'm so rattled by her comment that I don't even feel hurt by her insult.

Yoonie gives me a sympathetic smile. "I think your hair's cute. Very retro, very Sarah Michelle Gellar in *Grudge 2*. Who does your highlights?"

"No one. They're just like that. You know, naturally." I don't add that my mom cuts my hair, once a year. If I let her.

"No way! You're so lucky. I have to spend two hundred dollars a month to get this," Yoonie says.

"Big deal, sweetie, try *five* hundred a month," Priscilla scoffs.

"This hair talk is all very fascinating, but can we get back on topic? Money, people. I need money," Devon says irritably.

"Maybe we could throw a fund-raiser? Like a bake sale or something?" I suggest, wanting to be helpful. The Thorn Abbey boys must eat, even if the girls don't.

"I'm sure we'd be able to buy some *great* stuff with the twelve dollars we'd make from selling cupcakes," Devon says sarcastically.

I cringe. Devon seems to have gotten a lot more snitty since the subject of her mom came up. Or maybe she's upset about her parents' divorce. The other girls didn't seem surprised by the news. I guess she confides in them about family stuff, but not in me. On the other hand, I haven't confided in Devon about my family stuff either. Maybe if I open up to her, she'll open up to me?

It was so much easier at Avery Park High. Kayleigh was basically my only friend and we knew everything there was to know about each other's lives, and there was nothing to be embarrassed about because neither of our parents had money, fancy houses, glamorous jobs, or stable marriages. Besides, Kayleigh and I didn't have deep conversations. We mostly ate junk food and watched TV and strategized about her various unrequited crushes.

"I'll expect all contributions by end of next week. Then we can go shopping together that weekend," Devon announces.

"Isn't that the Corn Roast?" Priscilla asks.

"Oh. That." Devon picks up her phone and starts scrolling. "Hmm, you're right. No biggie, we can work around it."

"What's a Corn Roast?" I picture cobs of corn cooked on a giant spit, the way whole pigs are cooked at Hawaiian luaus.

"A big, huge party with a bonfire and barbecue and Headmaster Henle's old-person idea of 'pop music.' And, of course, a lot of drunken making out after dark when the grown-ups aren't looking," Yoonie says with a sly grin.

I picture myself at the Corn Roast with Max. Not that that would happen in a million years, but still. I dip my head and scarf down more tasteless vegetables so the other girls won't see me blush.

Devon is too focused to notice me. "Okay, next topic. There's a party in Chapin tonight. Eight o'clock, third floor, Killian Montgomery's room. You're all coming with me, right?"

Priscilla raises her hand. "Excuse me. Girls in Chapin? Without an official event? How are we supposed to get past the security guard and the house counselor?"

"Killian has that under control. We're supposed to tell the

guard we're going to a Movie Fest subcommittee meeting," Devon explains.

"Okay, well, count me in. As long as I can squeeze in a mani-pedi," Priscilla says, frowning at her nails.

"I'm in too, although I'll probably have to leave early. This cleanse is exhausting. I fainted in French yesterday, and Madame forced me to go see that bitch nurse, and she says I'm supposed to get more rest," Elinor mutters.

Yoonie checks her phone. "I've got chamber practice at seven thirty, but I can sneak out. It's just Mozart."

Devon nods approvingly. "Great. Tess? You're in too, right? It's time you got acquainted with Thorn Abbey's male population."

I stall, taking a long sip of lemon water. Eight o'clock is when I'm supposed to meet Max. "I can't."

"Why? Have you got a date?" Devon asks snidely.

I squirm. I can't tell her that I actually do have a date, with Max. She told me to stay away from him, and she isn't the sort of person one disobeys or says no to.

Back in Avery Park, I never got invited to parties. Now that I finally have one to go to, I'm desperate to get out of it. Ironic.

"I have this paper to write, and I haven't even started on it," I hedge.

Devon rolls her eyes. "Stop being such a colossal nerd. You *have* to come with us."

"I'll try. Just text me Kelly's room number, okay?"

"It's *Killian*."

"Sorry. Killian."

Devon glares at me suspiciously. I don't think she's buying my story about the paper. But she can't know I'm hanging out with Max, not after I promised her I wouldn't.

Although if Max and I continue to spend time together, how long am I going to be able to keep it a secret? I know it's wishful thinking to hope for anything more than study dates. But if my wish comes true, then what? Am I going to have to choose between Devon and Max?

Life at Thorn Abbey is *definitely* more complicated than life at Avery Park High.

12.

WHEN I GET TO THE LIBRARY AT 7:59 P.M., MAX IS ALREADY IN a secluded study nook. He texted me directions: second floor, through the mystery stacks, first desk on the right. Just beyond the Agatha Christies and Raymond Chandlers, I find him. Max's white button-down shirt, part of his school uniform, is untucked, and he's poring over an old book. Big swoon.

Love Poems from the Victorian Age is in curly gold script on the moss-green cover. He's reading love poems? Oh my God, double swoon.

I slide into the seat across from Max. "What're you reading?" I ask, as if I didn't know.

He looks up and smiles. "Hey! You're here!"

"I'm here."

He points to the book. "I thought I might use this poem in my paper for Bags."

Oh. So he wasn't planning on reading poetry as a way of declaring his love for me. "Who's it by?"

"I don't remember. I can't seem to find it, but I know it's in here somewhere."

He flips through the book, and the frail pages make a crackly, whispering sound. It feels so intimate, just him and me, our heads bent low as we study together by the warm glow of the brass desk lamps. I gaze at his face, at the way his dark, wavy hair falls across his forehead. And then there is that jagged scar on his cheek. I wonder how he got it. Maybe he took a spill on his bike when he was little?

I reach into my backpack and pull out my notebook, which I've neatly labeled *Tess Szekeres, Kerrith Hall*. I quickly open it to a clean page so Max doesn't see. He doesn't need to know that I live in Becca's old dorm. With Becca's old roommate. That would definitely kill the cozy, intimate mood.

"Have you come up with any ideas?" Max asks without looking up.

"For what?"

"For paper topics?"

Right. Mr. Bagley's assignment. Focus. "I was thinking of writing about existentialism in the novel," I tell him. "Or maybe something about the two endings—how the first one is a romantic nineteenth-century ending and the second one is a more realistic twentieth-century ending."

Max grins. "You should be teaching this class."

I blush. "Thanks."

"No, seriously. You're, like, the smartest girl I've ever met."

"Wow. Thanks." I wish I could tell him how *not* smart I've felt since coming to Thorn Abbey. How I'm clueless when it comes to Devon's and the other girls' favorite subjects, like diets and designer brands and so forth.

At least Max appreciates me for the stuff I *can* talk about.

"So what ideas have you come up with?" I ask him.

Max runs his hand through his hair. It sticks up this way and that, just like when we were on the cliff. When we almost kissed. I blush even more.

"Well, like I said, something based on the poem. If I can ever find it. If I'm remembering it right, the guy in the poem reminds me of Charles in the novel."

"In what way?"

"Charles is this upper-class Victorian guy and everyone expects him to behave a certain way, marry a certain kind of girl. But he rejects all that. Or tries to, anyway."

The way he says this—with a slight catch in his voice— makes me think he's somehow referring to himself. I bite my lip. If only I were smoother, more self-assured, I could draw him out and get him to confide in me. Is he from an upper-class family too? Do Max's parents expect a lot from him? I have no idea how to talk to a boy that way. I can barely manage the usual pleasantries without having a panic attack.

"That sounds terrific!" I say with more enthusiasm than I intended.

"You think so?" Max says eagerly. "I really respect your opinion on this." He stops flipping through the poetry book. "Found it! I knew it was in here. Okay, tell me if this sounds like a paper topic. It's short."

I smile. "I don't care if it's long. I don't have anywhere I have to be or anything like that."

He clears his throat and begins reading:

"This, he could not share with her, or any other soul.
Although at times, his secret felt not dark and wrong, but light
And true. But what was he to do? The laws of man said this.
His heart and mind said that. It was a contest for the gods
To weigh. Or for him to win with his fledgling wings and
    mortal faith."

He closes the book and gazes at me expectantly. "What do you think?"

My brain is buzzing and racing. I can't seem to formulate an articulate response. Being with Max, having him recite poetry to me . . . okay, so he wasn't reciting poetry to *me*, exactly, but it felt that way. His reading voice is so soft and deep and hypnotic, like a super-sexy lullaby. "What sort of secret are they . . . I mean he, the poet . . . talking about?" I sputter.

"I'm not sure. But it sounds like Charles, right?"

"Definitely!"

"I was also thinking about working Charles Darwin's ideas about evolution into my paper. Bags was talking about Darwin a lot today, remember? About the survival of the fittest? Maybe there's a way to connect all these themes." Max stands up. "Can you wait here? I'm going to go grab his book."

"*The Origin of Species?*"

"Yup, that's the one."

Max gets up and starts down the aisle. Before he disappears, he turns and flashes me a quick smile. I smile back. I may be imagining things, but I think he actually likes me. As in *likes* me.

My life is now complete.

Giggling happily, I pick up the book of love poems and begin leafing through it. Avery Park High would never have a cool old book like this in their library. Thorn Abbey's collection is definitely more impressive.

Except, it's not a library book. There is a handwritten inscription inside the front cover:

To Max
With all my love,
Becca

My chest tightens. I have forgotten how to breathe. Of course it was a gift from Becca. Of course Max still carries it around with him. How could I have thought that he liked me?

Becca must have been a really thoughtful and romantic girlfriend, giving a gift like that. Most girls I know would have chosen an iTunes card or a DVD instead. No wonder he was, is, in love with her.

I am so stupid.

With all my love, Becca. Even her handwriting is beautiful. And bold. The ink is a deep, velvety pink, the color of late-summer roses. Trembling, I touch the big, swirly *B* of her name . . .

. . . and recoil, stifling a scream. The page is burning hot.

But that's not possible. I touch it again, very, very gingerly. The page is cool and smooth, like one would expect.

I turn my hand over to look at my fingertips. They're bright red and raw and tender.

I must be going insane.

"I don't understand," I whisper.

"What don't you understand?"

Max has reappeared, a thick volume tucked under his arm. He stares at me curiously. "Are you okay? You look like you saw a ghost."

"I'm fine. Here's your book back." I slide it across the desk to him. It's haunted. *He's* haunted. I grab my notebook and backpack. "I have to go."

"What? You just got here. Besides, I was hoping I could bounce more ideas off you. We could take a walk, if you'd like?"

"I can't."

I bolt out without saying good-bye. He must think I'm crazy.

Maybe I *am* crazy.

What is happening to me?

13.

OUTSIDE, THE AIR IS THICK AND HUMID, LIKE A WET SLICKER that sticks to your skin. My mom always complains about September weather because it can be hot one day and freezing the next. It's probably going to start raining at any moment now, and I don't have an umbrella.

I hurry through the quad, wondering which way I should go. Back to Kerrith? I might run into Devon and the others, and they would force me to go to that party. Over to Lanyon, so I can hang out in the computer center and creep on a dead girl some more?

I think I'm losing my mind.

Why did I ever come to Thorn Abbey, anyway?

I choke back a sob. *Great.* On top of everything, I'm going to have a PMS meltdown in the middle of campus. I pass a group of seniors walking toward the library. They stare at me, and one of them says, "Yeah, that's that girl who—"

"Tess! Wait up!"

I turn. Max is jogging in my direction. It didn't occur to me that he might follow me.

He stops in front of me. He looks worried, or mad, or both. It's hard to tell. "What's wrong?" he demands.

"Nothing!" I say, quickly blinking back tears.

"You're lying. What happened while I was in the stacks?"

"Nothing."

Max crosses his arms over his chest. "Seriously, stop lying."

I purse my lips together stubbornly. I can't tell him that I saw Becca's inscription. Or that it made me insanely jealous. Or that it made me insane, *period*, because somehow, I imagined that her signature burned my fingers, and they actually throbbed with pain. Isn't there some mental illness where you hallucinate an injury and your body reacts with real symptoms? That's me.

I don't know why Max almost kissed me on the cliff or why he asked me to hang out with him tonight. Maybe he was just lonely. Or bored. Whatever the reason, I've had enough. He's not the one who needs to move on. I am.

"Tess." Max starts to reach for me, then drops his arms to

his sides. "I don't know what to do. Is it just me, or are we always chasing each other across campus?"

On Monday night, I chased out of the movie after him. On Tuesday morning, I chased after him before he could jump off a cliff. So far, I'm the one who's done most of the chasing. "So?"

"Maybe we should stop running away and, well, just stop running."

"Why?" I ask skeptically.

"So we can be friends?"

"Why would we want to do that?"

"Because." He laughs awkwardly. "Why are you making this hard for me?"

Because I don't want to be a fool anymore. "Hard for you how?"

"Look. I don't have a lot of close friends. I have one, to be exact. Franklin. It's not easy for me to"—Max stuffs his hands into his pockets—"What would my shrink say? Open up."

I melt a little inside. Max is confiding in me. "I can relate to that."

"You can?"

"Definitely. I'd rather eat dirt than talk about myself."

He smiles.

"I've never been in therapy. What's it like?" I ask curiously.

"You'd hate it. You have to talk about yourself the whole time."

I smile. "What's your therapist like?"

"I don't see him anymore. My parents made me go, after—"
He hesitates.

Oh, God. Me and my big mouth. "I'm sorry. I didn't mean
to—"

"No, it's okay."

Max falls silent. I am *such* a moron. He finally tells me
something personal, and I remind him of Becca and make him
clam up.

I don't know what to do. What if Max is being sincere? I
want him to like me the way I like him. But then I think of
Becca's inscription. I wish I could ask him why he still has that
book of love poems. There could be a totally innocent explanation. Like, it was gathering dust on his shelf until he decided to
use it for his English paper, and he doesn't even remember that
it was a gift from Becca.

I tilt my head to the sky. But there are no answers or epiph-
anies up there. Just rain clouds.

A couple of girls pass by, chattering about the Corn Roast.
"Hey, Max!" they call out in unison. He barely acknowledges
them, even though they're drop-dead gorgeous. He's watching
me intently.

I meet his gaze. "Why do you want to hang out with me?"
I ask him bluntly.

"What? Where's this coming from?" he says, sounding surprised.

"I'm nothing like"—I catch myself—"like the other girls at Thorn Abbey. I'm not beautiful and rich and sophisticated. I grew up in a town full of meth labs and cheap nail salons. I didn't know what a Burberry was. I had to look it up."

"Tess—"

"You don't need to feel sorry for me because I'm the new girl," I rush on, trying to mask the hurt in my voice. "I'm not a charity case. You don't need to feel like you owe me because of what happened on the cliff. We're not in a *Star Trek: Voyager* episode, where it's like, 'Oh, you saved my life, so now I'm obligated to follow you across the Delta Quadrant and be your personal servant forever,' blah, blah, blah."

Max grins. *"Tess!"* he repeats loudly.

"What?"

He cradles my face with his hand. "Listen. I like you *because* you're not like the other girls here. Most of them only care about clothes, money, stupid shit like that. You're nice, and you're real. You say what's on your mind. You don't worry about what other people think of you."

"Well, actually, I do worry." But it's hard to get the words out, or articulate anything at all, because his hand is still touching my face, and his incredible brown eyes are staring into mine. Plus I'm frantically trying to process everything he's said to me.

"You shouldn't care about other people," Max says fiercely. "Most of them are idiots. And fakes. They pretend to be something they're not just to get what they want, and—"

"Well, hello, you two!"

Startled, I glance past Max. Oh, God. Devon is strolling toward us with a big, mean smile on her face.

This is not good.

"Tess. Max. Fancy running into you here," Devon says sweetly. She is wearing a crazy-short red dress and ridiculously high heels. Why is she wearing a Las Vegas call girl outfit? Then I remember that party at Chapin.

Max pulls away from me, as though we're strangers suddenly. "Devon. I was just heading back to my dorm."

"Oh, please don't leave on my account! You lovebirds looked so cozy!" she trills.

Max doesn't reply, just glares at her. He is a different person from a moment ago: ice-cold, hostile. Why is he acting like this? I thought he and Devon were friends.

"I didn't know you knew each other," he says to me in a low, tense voice.

What is going on? I open my mouth to speak, wondering how I'm going to explain. But as always, Devon beats me to the punch. "Oh, Tess didn't tell you? We're roommates."

Max's jaw drops. "Excuse me?"

"Yup, we're practically BFFs. Aren't we, Tess? And you know me, Max. I've already got her on a crash course to shed those extra pounds and trailer-park habits. Pretty soon, she'll be the queen of Kerrith Hall. Right, Tess?"

My face grows hot. I'm so uncomfortable and embarrassed, I can't even respond. Why is Devon being so mean?

"Did you finish that paper you were telling me about? We can walk over to Killian's party together. We'll be fashionably late. Max, join us?"

"Yeah, I don't think so," Max replies tersely.

"Suit yourself. Come on, Tess."

"Go on without me. I'll catch up with you," I say quickly.

Devon raises an eyebrow. I can tell she's pissed. But her scarlet-red mouth curves into an indulgent smile, indicating otherwise. Or maybe it's her way of telling me that she'll deal with me later.

"Alrighty, then. Have fun! Don't do anything I wouldn't do. Max, a pleasure, as always."

She blows a kiss and takes off. She disappears down the path, somehow managing to strut like a runway model in her pointy four-inch heels.

Silence.

"Max—"

"So you know, obviously, that Devon and Becca were room-mates," Max cuts in.

I nod meekly.

"Is that why you didn't mention Devon before?"

"I thought it might be awkward. I didn't want to hurt your feelings or bring back bad memories or anything like that."

"Bad memories?" he says incredulously. "So is that how you knew about me and Becca? Because Devon told you?"

"Y-yes."

He laughs bitterly. "Yeah, that's great."

"Max, I'm really sorry if I—"

He holds up his hands and starts walking away. "No, don't be sorry. Enjoy your party. Good-bye, Tess."

"I'm not—"

But he was already gone.

14.

THAT NIGHT, I LIE IN BED, TRYING TO RE-CREATE THAT PERFECT minute and a half when Max was touching my face and gazing soulfully into my eyes. For those ninety seconds, he liked me. For those ninety seconds, we were almost more than friends.

Why does something always come between us?

Devon isn't home yet. She must still be at that party. Outside, a steady rain drums against the window. The room feels damp and smells faintly of perfume, although it's not the musky one Devon usually wears. It's sweet, floral, and feminine. It must be her perfume for special occasions.

I like you because you're not like the other girls here.

Why did Max like Becca? Not just *like* her, but love her? I wish I could find out more about her so I could understand him better. Maybe someday he will trust me enough to tell me about their relationship. If he ever talks to me again, that is.

Better yet, maybe I will come to my senses and fall for a boy who isn't haunted by the memory of his ex-girlfriend. Why can't I be attracted to a nice, available boy like, say, Franklin? I could be wrong, but I think he likes me.

Above my head, something taps and scrapes against the other side of the ceiling. I burrow under my comforter.

Tap . . . tap tap tap.

Tap . . . tap tap tap.

The noise gets louder. I poke my head out.

Tap . . . tap tap tap.

Tap . . . tap tap tap.

I hold my breath and listen intently. It's as though someone—or something—is trying to break through the ceiling.

And then I remember.

There *is* no fourth floor in Kerrith.

The noise grows louder, then softer, then louder again. *It must be the rain on the roof*, I tell myself nervously.

My heart racing, I hug my pillow to my chest and burrow under the comforter again. "Monday September second, Monday September ninth, Monday September sixteenth," I whisper under my breath.

⚜ ⚜ ⚜

I startle awake in the middle of the night to find Devon beside me, stroking my hair.

"You poor baby," she whispers.

I try to sit up. But she puts her hand on my chest, just firmly enough so that I can't move. Her makeup is smeared, and her lips are puffy and bare. Her red minidress is wrinkled and reeks of beer. What in the hell is going on? Is she drunk, or is she having one of her sleep-talking spells again?

She has turned on my yellow smiley-face lamp, and I feel, eerily, as though I am in an interrogation room.

"You poor, poor baby. You have no idea what you've gotten yourself into, do you?" Devon croons. "Do you know who the De Villierses are?"

I blink. "What?"

"I didn't think so. They're one of the richest, most powerful families in New York City."

"They are?" I rub my eyes, trying to comprehend what she is saying.

"Mm-hmm. Mr. De Villiers runs ten different corporations, and Mrs. De Villier's father is a US senator. They sit on all the most important boards; they're invited to absolutely every social event that matters. They're royalty, basically."

I sort of guessed that Max came from a wealthy family, but I didn't realize they were like the Kennedys. Still, why is

Devon telling me this at two a.m.? And why is she acting like a crazy person? She's seriously freaking me out.

"Max is the heir to the throne," she says in a faraway voice, her hand still pressing against my chest. "I've met Mr. and Mrs. De Villiers, and they can be a bit . . . intimidating. They're not going to be happy when they find out their son is hooking up with you."

"But we aren't—"

"Can't you see that he's using you to get over his grief? That you're just a distraction? All the other girls know to keep their distance after what happened. He's an emotional train wreck, and he needs time. Friends. Not some love-starved loner throwing herself at him."

"But I'm not—"

"Becca told me that he tries to put on this act, like he's so cool and above it all. But deep down, he's really vulnerable. Romantic. Do you know that he proposed to her?" she sneers.

"E-excuse me?" I'm not just freaked out anymore. I feel sick to my stomach.

"I don't mean he gave her a ring or anything like that. But he told her that he wanted to marry her someday." Devon smiles wistfully, as if she's reliving a memory. "Becca was so excited. We even looked at wedding dress websites together, for fun. She picked out this amazing gown. She was so gorgeous, she could get married in sweats and get away with it. You saw her picture, so you know what I'm talking about, right?" She gives my chest a little shove and pulls away.

"R-right." This is a nightmare. Literally a nightmare. I'm going to wake up any second now.

Devon trails her fingers across my bed. "You know, she used to beg me to let her have the room Saturday nights so they could be alone," she says dreamily. "She had all kinds of creative ways of sneaking him in here."

In here. Wait. Was she saying . . .

"You mean, this room was your old room . . . with Becca?" I whisper.

"Of course. They insisted on giving me a different one, because of the circumstances. But I didn't want it. This was Becca's favorite room in Kerrith, and mine, too. It's the biggest, and it has the best view. Besides, I feel closer to her here."

Oh, God. Now I *really* feel sick. I'm living in Becca's old room. And probably even sleeping in Becca's old bed.

The bed where she and Max used to . . .

Devon bends down. "I'm not going to tell you to stop hanging out with Max," she murmurs in my ear, her black hair splaying across my face like a million fine needles. "But you shouldn't let him use you like this. You're a real catch, and you deserve soooo much better."

☙ ☙ ☙

The next morning, I wake up to my phone. I must have a voice mail or a text message. It keeps beeping, beeping.

I hoist myself on my elbows, groggily fighting the nasty cobwebs in my head. I wonder if this is what a hangover feels like. Not that I would know, since the only alcohol I've ever had is communion wine at church and the two sips of Budweiser that Kayleigh forced me to try once.

Across the room, Devon is lying facedown on her bed, wearing only her panties. Her red dress lies crumpled on the floor.

Her silver box sits on the pillow next to her head. The one containing Becca's photo.

You poor, poor baby. You have no idea what you've gotten yourself into, do you?

My chest tightens. I reach for my stupid phone. There is a text message—no, two text messages.

They are both from Max.

I frown. What could he possibly want from me? His goodbye seemed so final.

He's an emotional train wreck, and he needs time. Friends. Not some love-starved loner throwing herself at him.

Surely, Devon was wasted. Surely, she didn't know what she was saying.

I take a deep breath and open the first message.

Sorry about last night.

A tentative smile spreads across my face. So Max and I *aren't* through.

Heart racing, I open the second message.

Do you want to go to the Corn Roast with me next Saturday?

I read the message again. And again. Is he asking me out on a date?

Can't you see that he's using you to get over his grief? That you're just a distraction?

My smile vanishes. I chew on my thumbnail.

She used to beg me to let her have the room Saturday nights so they could be alone.

I curl up in a ball, clutching my phone. An image of Becca and Max flashes in my mind, their naked bodies intertwined.

"Stop it," I whisper miserably. "Stop it stop it stop it."

I lift the phone to my face and type a response to Max, then hit send before I can change my mind.

Yes.

15.

On the night of the Corn Roast, I take forever to get ready for my date with Max. I try on six tops before I finally settle on a baby-blue sweater Kayleigh picked out for me at the mall. She said it made me look "a tiny bit slutty," which I'm not so sure is a good thing. But Devon isn't here to give me a second opinion, and I don't want to be late.

Heading out the door, I'm nervous and excited. Besides English, I haven't seen much of Max in the last week and a half. He walked me to Latin a few times, and we talked about easy, neutral things like homework and student elections. Becca's name didn't come up, not even once. Neither did Devon's. He told me about a project he had to do for chemistry, plus a couple of big soccer games. I guess that was his way of saying he didn't have time to hang out.

Which makes it even more special that we're together tonight. Special and anxiety producing. On the one hand, I like him and I want him to like me. On the other hand, I hope I didn't make a mistake, agreeing to this date. Is he truly over Becca?

You have no idea what you've gotten yourself into.

I still can't get that creepy conversation with Devon out of my head.

Devon was like a crazy possessed person that night. Then, the next morning, she acted like nothing had happened. I'm actually a little worried about her. Her sleep-talking spells have become more frequent and intense. Last Saturday, I woke up to find her having an angry conversation with the ceiling. It lasted an entire hour.

I wonder if *she* has a therapist? Maybe I should talk to the girls.

Max is waiting for me on the bench by the fountain. He looks really handsome in a faded gray T-shirt, black jeans, and leather jacket. His hair is slightly damp, like he just showered. My palms are actually sweaty, which never happens to me—

except once, when I had to play a solo at the honors band concert because the first clarinet was out sick.

Max's head is bent low, and he is texting intently. When he sees me, he stands up and tucks his phone into his jacket pocket. It's the same jacket he was wearing in that photo with Becca, on the school website.

"Hey." He smiles at me, although his eyes look tired.

"Hi." I smile back, trying not to feel weird about the jacket. I mean, what's he supposed to do—not wear it just because he's on a date with me and not Becca? "I'm psyched about this Corn Roast!" I say in a fake-cheerful voice.

"Don't be. It's kind of lame. But I'm glad you're here, anyway." He wraps his arm around my waist. "Shall we?"

We start across the quad toward Hunters' Meadow. He keeps his arm where it is, which is a good sign, I think—physical contact. Then his phone starts buzzing, and he reaches in his jacket and turns it off. Who was he texting? Who is texting him back?

Cut it out, I tell myself. *Just relax and have fun.*

The entire Thorn Abbey population seems to be gathered at Hunters' Meadow, including students, teachers, and random employees. There is a massive fire pit in the middle of the sprawling green lawn, and the air is thick with the aroma of roasting corn. A couple of ancient rock-concert-size speakers blast a Journey song that I recognize from my mom's aerobics playlist. Wow, Yoonie was right about Headmaster Henle's taste in music. Some of the seniors are playing Ultimate Frisbee in the waning twilight.

I scan the rest of the crowd. I recognize a bunch of girls from Kerrith. There is no sign of Devon, though—or Priscilla or Elinor or Yoonie, for that matter. They drove into town after lunch to shop for the lounge project, and they must not be back yet. Maybe, if I'm lucky, they'll miss the Corn Roast altogether and I won't have to deal with Devon's weirdness about me being with Max.

Or Max's weirdness about her. I wish I could ask him about it, but I'm afraid it will put him in a bad mood. He seems distant and distracted as it is.

"Soooo. Where's Franklin?" I ask.

"What?" His face is pensive, like he's mulling over a problem. "Yeah, he texted me. I think he's coming by later."

"Oh. So what's next? Do we sit around the fire and eat corn?"

Max nods. "That pretty much covers it. It's always the same drill. Last year, it rained the whole time, so the bonfire was a fail."

Last year. I picture him and Becca holding hands and kissing in the rain. Sneaking away for a drunk make-out session. *No, no, don't think about that.*

"Tess?" He looks at me with a puzzled expression. "Everything okay?"

"I'm fine. Let's get some food."

We wind our way toward the catering tables, where we grab paper plates and utensils and start down the line. The boy in front of us turns around. He's wearing a T-shirt that says BOLLINGER FOR PRESIDENT.

"Hey, guys! Welcome! Ben Bollinger," he says, grabbing my hand and shaking it vigorously.

"Hi, Ben. I'm Tess."

"Nice to meet you, Tess. Listen, Max. I know Ayesha's already bugged you, but I wanted to make my pitch. You and me. Junior-class president and vice president."

"Thanks, I'm flattered. But my schedule's pretty full," Max says apologetically.

"Yeah, I thought you'd say that. But definitely next year, okay? With your family's reputation, we'd be unbeatable."

Max's family's reputation. Devon may have been drunk, but she wasn't kidding about the De Villierses. The other day, I overhead someone in my American history class saying that Max's great-grandfather used to be secretary of state.

I've never known anyone from such a prominent family. The closest I ever came was probably Tiffani Camacho, whose cousin was on *American Idol*.

At the first station, Mila Kunis is in charge of ladling out coleslaw. When she spots Max and me, she gives us a big smile. "Hi, you two! Tess, I like your sweater! Where did you get it?" she chirps.

Mila Kunis knows my name? And she likes my sweater? This is the first time she has spoken to me, ever. "It was a Christmas present," I say, which sounds better than "a deep clearance bin at Boscov's."

"Cool. That color's really pretty on you."

"Thanks." I'm surprised and pleased that Mila Kunis recognized *and* complimented me. *Huh.* Maybe I'm not the school outcast after all.

Except, one of the mean blond Kerrith girls is at the next station, serving the hot dogs. I can feel my shoulders tense up. Is she going to say something nasty?

But shockingly, she smiles at me too. "Do you want a real hot dog or one of these vomitacious vegan ones? Oops, sorry, you're not a vegan, are you?" she says in a friendly voice.

"Um, no. I'll take a real one."

"Excellent choice. My parents are vegans. I like to bring home burgers from the BK Lounge, just to mess with them."

The BK Lounge?

"Burger King," Max whispers in my ear. He must have seen the confusion on my face.

"Thanks," I whisper back gratefully.

"Guys, a little consideration? We're starving back here," a girl in the back of the line complains.

"I'm sorry. We're holding things up," I apologize to the Kerrith girl.

"No worries. I don't know why Savannah's in such a mad rush for food. Seriously, she gained like twenty pounds over the summer." She plops a hot dog on my plate. "Enjoy!"

"Yo, Max! Tess!" Nate says, passing by.

"Max, that was a sweet goal today!" another boy calls out. "Hey, Tess, right? Welcome to Thorn Abbey!"

Why is everyone being so nice to me all of a sudden? Oh, yeah. I'm with Max. In a school full of privileged A-list kids, he's way up there on the social ladder. Which makes me, his date for the Corn Roast, up there too. At least for tonight.

The thing is, Max doesn't seem to care much about being popular. I guess that's one of the things I like about him.

He and I take our food and find a spot that's close but not too close to the bonfire. We sit down on the grass and balance our plates on our laps. I take a bite of my hot dog. Not awful. Actually, pretty yummy, compared to the raw vegetable and broth diet Devon's forced on me.

"So your family's pretty involved in politics, huh?" I ask Max. "Your grandfather's a senator, right?"

"Yup. Jorge Salazar."

"Oh! Senator Salazar! I've seen him on TV."

Max doesn't respond. He spears a deviled egg with his fork but doesn't eat it. He doesn't seem too interested in eating. Or our conversation, for that matter.

"So are you and your grandfather close?" I persist.

"Yeah, when I was little. He's pretty busy these days."

"He must be. I read that he's working on a bill about tougher penalties for texting while driving."

"Hmm."

He lapses into silence again. He turns and stares intently at the bonfire. Its flames glow orange against the darkening sky.

And then it hits me. He doesn't want to be here. With me. He's probably remembering last year's Corn Roast, when he was with Becca. Miss Sophomore-Class President. They obviously had politics in common, among other things.

The knowledge tears me up inside and makes me want to cry. I curl my hands into fists and try to decide if I should make up an excuse and leave.

"My dad used to build bonfires on the beach," Max says, out of the blue.

I glance at him in surprise. My hands relax slightly.

"We have this place on the Vineyard. Every Labor Day, my parents have this big party and invite everyone we know. My *abuelo*, my grandfather, never misses it. He'll fly up from DC for the day if he has to. My dad builds a bonfire, and we have lobsters, clams, corn . . . the whole bit."

"That sounds amazing," I say. Is he talking about Martha's Vineyard? I wonder if he ever brought Becca there.

"Yeah, well, I didn't go to the Vineyard at all this summer. Dad was in Europe a lot, on business. I could have gone with my mom or my grandparents or Franklin, but . . ." He shakes his head. "I didn't feel like being at the beach. After what happened. I wanted to stay in the city. The skyscrapers and the noise, they felt safer to me than . . . you know. That's messed up, right?"

Oh my gosh. Poor Max.

"It's not messed up at all. It makes perfect sense," I say softly.

He smiles and slips his hand into mine. His fingers are warm and strong. My heart knocks in my chest. I was wrong about him. He's opening up to me. He wants to move on.

To hell with Rebecca Rose Winters.

I almost don't see the bright, tiny spark flying through the air toward me. It arcs neatly, almost deliberately, over the cluster of people sitting in front of Max and me and lands directly on my sleeve.

The fabric smolders, then crackles into flame. My sweater

is on fire. For a second, I'm too stunned to react. And then I jump to my feet, screaming.

"Tess, get down!" Max yells.

My skin burns as fire rushes up my arm. Max tackles me to the ground. He rolls me over and over on the dewy grass. The flame dies out with an angry, defeated hiss.

"Are you okay?" Max demands breathlessly.

I can barely find my voice. "I think so?"

Trembling, I touch my sweater. The sleeve is perfectly intact. There are no holes or singed threads.

What the hell?

I roll up my sleeve and touch the skin on my arm gingerly. It doesn't hurt, and there's no mark whatsoever.

"This doesn't make any sense," I say out loud.

"What doesn't make any sense? Tess, talk to me," Max pleads.

People gather around us, whispering and buzzing.

"Miss Szekeres, are you all right?" It's Headmaster Henle.

"Yes, I'm fine," I reply. *Fine but extremely confused.*

"I'd like you to see the nurse. Mr. De Villiers, can you escort her to the clinic?"

"Yes, sir."

Max grasps my hand and gently lifts me to my feet. He takes off his leather jacket and drapes it around my shoulders.

As we walk, I overhear snippets of hushed conversations:

"Who's that girl with Max?"

"He used to date Becca Winters, right?"

"Did you see what happened?"

"Looked like one of those Molotov cocktails from Grand Theft Auto."

"She was sitting too close to the fire."

"No, they were sitting way in back. It must have been the wind."

But there is no wind.

And my sweater and arm are totally unscathed. It's like nothing ever happened.

Max holds me tightly and kisses my hair. "Are you sure you're okay?"

"I'm sure."

That's when I catch sight of Devon standing at the edge of the crowd. When did she get here?

And why is she smiling at me? Not her dazzling smile, but a different smile, like she's in crazy mode again.

I shudder and start to turn away.

Then, for a split second, her entire body glows white.

Just like that seagull.

16.

I HAVE TO TALK TO SOMEONE. ANYONE.

When I get back from the clinic, Devon isn't in our room. Thank God. I need privacy, and besides, I don't think I can deal with her glow-in-the-dark weirdness right now.

I lie down on my bed and call Kayleigh. Or RYAN GOSLING, as she input herself in my contact list. I honestly don't know who else to turn to. I don't feel close enough to anyone at Thorn Abbey. Not even Max, who'd probably think I was delusional if I told him about this stuff.

Kayleigh picks up on the first ring, even though it's late. *"TESSIE!"* she practically screams into the phone. "Ohmigod, how are you? Why are you calling me? You *never* call me. Are you in trouble?"

"Hi, K. No, I'm not in trouble." I pause. "Well, maybe just a little."

"I *knew* it. I was literally thinking about you *this second*. My psychic abilities always go insane with the full moon."

"Uh. Okay. Listen. Something strange happened to me tonight. And . . ."

"Spill."

I tell Kayleigh about the flying ember and how it burned me but didn't burn me. I also tell her about Devon flashing fluorescent, and the seagull, too.

When I'm finished, she says, "Ohmigod. That's totally *Ghost Town*."

"What's that?"

"It's only the most awesome TV show ever. Is Thane Abby old? Could it be haunted?"

"No. What I mean is, yes, it's old, but no, I don't think it's haunted."

"Don't be so sure. Has anything else happened? Anything supernatural, that is?"

I consider this. My second day here, I imagined that someone snuck up on me from behind on the Kerrith stairs, making me fall. When I was at the library with Max, I imagined that Becca's signature scorched my fingers. Then there was the tapping.

And Devon's sleep-talking spells. And the crying from Gita's room.

I relay all this to Kayleigh.

"If you want my opinion? I think we're talking serious paranormal activity," Kayleigh says when I'm finished. "Unless it's drugs. You haven't gotten into drugs, have you?"

"No!"

"Don't be so touchy! I'm just asking. What about your roommate? Is *she* on something."

"Maybe?"

"Although that wouldn't explain the glowing. I don't know of any drugs that make you glow. I'll have to Wikipedia that."

"Okay."

"Listen, Tess. I'll research all this for you and get back to you. Do you have a cat's-eye?"

"A *what?*" I picture a dead cat's eye. *Gross.*

"Cat's-eye. Peridot would work too. They're gemstones that provide protection against evil. Check online. There's a site called the Magikal Owl that has awesome stuff. That's 'Magikal' with a *k*."

"I will," I say, although I doubt I'll be shopping at the Magikal Owl anytime soon. "Thanks."

"You're welcome. Be safe, please? And call me like *immediately* if anything else happens."

"I will. Bye, Kayleigh."

"Bye, Tessie."

I hang up and start getting ready for bed. I do feel a little better after talking with Kayleigh. It was good to hear a familiar, friendly voice.

Not that I buy any of her ideas about the supernatural. I don't believe in ghosts or cat's-eyes or any of this occult stuff.

On the other hand, what other explanation is there?

17.

At 7:20 on Monday night, I rush into Chapin, chomping on a breath mint and swiping stray strands of hair out of my face. I'm running late. I was supposed to meet Max in the lobby five minutes ago so we could walk into tonight's movie together: *Double Indemnity*, starring Barbara Stanwyck and Fred MacMurray.

I left Devon in our room, studying for a Spanish quiz. She's been acting normal since the Corn Roast. Normal for Devon, anyway. She didn't come home that night. Yesterday, she showed up around noon wearing her same clothes. She called me an "accident magnet" and asked me if I was okay after the bonfire incident. She also updated me on the lounge project. But that was all.

NANCY OHLIN

Maybe Kayleigh is right. Maybe Devon's got a drug problem. That would explain so much.

Max is not in the lobby. I reach into my pocket for my phone to text him. It's not there. It's not in my backpack, either. *Ugh.* Did I leave it on the charger again?

"Looking for someone?"

An extremely cute blond guy stands in the doorway to the parlors. He has a slight British accent. Something about the way he looks at me—like I'm a fascinating insect or a particularly tasty snack—makes me blush.

"I, uh . . . no. I mean, yes. I'm meeting Max. Max De Villiers."

He smiles affably. "Oh, you're waiting for Maxi! You must be the new girlfriend. Lucky guy."

Now I'm *definitely* blushing. "I'm Tess."

He walks up to me and takes my hand. He raises it to his lips and kisses it lightly. "Killian. Killian Montgomery. I'm sure Maxi's told you all about me."

His name sounds familiar. "I don't think so."

"Really? I'm very offended. Let me keep you company while you wait for him." Killian leads me by the hand to a blue velvet couch in the corner. Hanging above it is a painting of men on horseback chasing some poor little fox. At the moment, I can kind of relate to the fox. "So! You're new, aren't you? Where are you from? What do you think of our quaint little

114

school? I'm sorry, I'm barraging you with questions, aren't I?"

"Not at all." Killian is still holding my hand. I gently pull it away and pretend to retie my ponytail. The front door opens and closes as a group of students make their way to the parlors for the movie, but no Max. "I'm from upstate. New York, that is. Thorn Abbey is really nice. It's—" I pause, trying to figure out what I can say that won't make me sound like a school brochure.

But before I can go on, Killian cuts in. "It's full of trust-fund babies and backstabbing bitches? I couldn't agree with you more. Of course, if I had to be perfectly honest, I probably fall into one or both categories. But don't hold that against me. I promise you, we're going to be best friends."

"We are?"

"We are. Wait, didn't I hear about a demonic fireball attacking you at the hoedown on Saturday? Have you recovered? You certainly *look* perky."

A demonic fireball. Killian's description is eerily accurate. "I'm fine," I say. It's the same thing I've been repeating to people for the past two days.

"Well, good! I got to the party late and missed all the drama. And speaking of parties, why weren't you at mine?"

"Your party?"

"Two Wednesdays ago. It was quite the scene. A room full

of the aforementioned trust-fund babies and backstabbing bitches trying to out-rich and out-bitch each other. It was titillating."

"Oh." So *that's* why his name sounded familiar. It was his party Devon wanted me to go to. Max refused to stop by, though. I wonder why, especially if he and Killian are supposedly friends?

"I host these little soirees regularly. Of course you'll be at the next one," Killian says.

"Well, I'm not sure if—"

"Good. It's settled. Speaking of trust-fund babies, where *is* that Maximilian? It's incredibly rude of him to keep you waiting like this. Doesn't he know it's dangerous for a lovely girl like you to be out and about on her own? Someone might snatch you up."

Lovely girl? Me?

The front door opens, and this time, Franklin walks in. He frowns when he spots the two of us on the couch. "Tess! Good, I was looking for you," he says, ignoring Killian.

"You were?"

Killian puts his arm around my shoulders. "Well, you're too late, Chase. She's mine until your lord and master gets here. Aren't you, Tess?"

"Very funny, Montgomery. Tess, can I talk to you? Alone?"

"Sure." I rise to my feet. What's up with Killian and Franklin? "Nice to meet you, Killian."

"The pleasure was all mine." Killian winks at me.

Franklin takes my elbow and nudges me in the direction of the parlors. "I'd advise you to stay away from him," he whispers.

"Oh, really? First you tell me to stay away from Max. Now it's Killian. Don't you want me to have any friends?" I snap.

"Yes, of course I do. But if I were you, I wouldn't tell Max that you were hanging out with Killian."

"What? Why not?"

He sighs. "It's complicated. Listen, Max texted me and asked me to find you. He said he tried to call you, but you didn't pick up. "

"I left my cell in my room. Is he okay?"

"He can't make it tonight. He's not feeling well."

"Oh." I try to shrug off my disappointment.

"I'm going to the movie, though. Do you want to sit together?"

"Um, sure." I force myself to sound enthusiastic. I do like Franklin. I just wish he were Max instead.

As Franklin and I walk into the parlors, I wonder why Killian wants to be my new best friend. Unless he was just being charming and over the top. Maybe that's how British boys act.

I also wonder why I'm not supposed to mention him to Max. Is it my imagination, or are there a lot of rules and secrets swirling around this place? Devon doesn't want me to date Max. Franklin doesn't want me to either. Max seems to have an issue with Devon. He also seems to have an issue with Killian, at least according to Franklin. And there was a weird vibe between Franklin and Killian, too.

It's like eighth grade all over again, except that the stakes feel way higher.

After the movie, Franklin and I sit on the front steps of Chapin snacking on candy bars from the vending machine. I'm sure Devon wouldn't approve, but I can't help it. I'm pretty much starving on my broth and salad regime, although my jeans are fitting a little looser these days.

"So what did you think?" Franklin asks me.

"It was creepy. But awesome. Nothing like a woman who seduces a guy, convinces him to help her kill her husband for the insurance money, and all while she is hooking up with her stepdaughter's boyfriend." I laugh and take a bite of my Almond Joy. "I actually saw it once before on TMC, with my mom."

"Me too. There's this theater in Astoria that shows old movies."

"Astoria. That's across the river from Manhattan, right? In Queens? Is that where you're from?" I ask.

"Yes."

"You said you grew up with Max. Is he from Astoria, too?"

Franklin chuckles. "No. The De Villierses live on the Upper East Side. My dad works for Max's father. Dad used to bring me to the office sometimes when I was little. That's how I met Max."

"Oh!" I had no idea their families were connected that way.

"Max went to Beardsley, a very exclusive day school. I went to PS 439. The thing is, I got picked on a lot there. So Mr. De Villiers pulled some strings and got me admitted to Beardsley, with a full scholarship. I didn't get picked on there because I was Max's best friend. No one messed with him because he was this big, tall kid and—I don't know, people just didn't mess with him. He and I were there through eighth grade. Then Max came to Thorn Abbey, and Mr. De Villiers pulled more strings and got me a full scholarship here."

"Wow. That's nice of Max's dad to help you like that."

Franklin shrugs. "He did it for Max. Max liked me, and he didn't have a lot of close friends."

"Why do you think that is?"

"I don't know. He's kind of guarded. Private. But you probably know that already."

Max told me that he had a hard time opening up. It sounds like he's always been this way.

A group of students walks by, debating the merits of San Andreas versus Liberty City. Franklin watches them, then crumples his candy bar wrapper and stuffs it into his backpack. "So the two of you are dating now," he says without looking at me.

"D-did he tell you that?" I feel at once pleased and anxious. I like thinking of Max thinking of me that way. On the other hand, I don't want another lecture from Franklin.

"It's kind of obvious," he replies testily.

I can't tell if Franklin is annoyed with me for ignoring his advice, or jealous, or worried for Max, or what. Although maybe I'm flattering myself with the "jealous" thing.

"I guess we're kind of dating. I'm not sure," I admit. "Can I ask you something?"

He nods.

"That day when you ran into me in the computer center? You said I should stay away from Max because he had issues."

"Yes."

"What kind of issues?"

Franklin hesitates. "Issues having to do with Becca," he says finally. "You could call it unfinished business. He's not exactly in a position to be in a relationship with anyone right now."

"Oh." *Ouch.* If anyone knows if Max still has feelings for Becca, it would be Franklin, right?

"Obviously, I can't stop you. Or him, for that matter. But I don't want to see you get hurt," Franklin goes on.

"Oh." I finish off my candy bar and immediately wish I had another one. "Hey, Franklin?"

"What?"

"What was Becca like?"

His eyes get a faraway look. "She was incredibly popular. And very beautiful. It was hard for anyone to resist her."

I'm sorry I asked.

18.

BACK IN OUR ROOM, DEVON IS LYING ON MY BED, SCROLLING through my phone.

"What are you doing?" I dump my backpack on the floor and hold out my hand. "Give me that. That's mine!"

Devon glares at me and tosses the phone in my direction. "Yeah, I know it's yours, dumb ass. I'm trying to figure out how to make it stop beeping. I can't get any studying done."

Oh, God, how embarrassing. "I'm sorry."

"What model is this, anyway? It's like from 1995. You need to upgrade."

"Sorry."

I check my phone. There are several texts and missed calls from Max. I glance at the first text:

Sorry. I can't make it tonight. Migraine.

Devon rises to her feet and saunters over to her own bed. Her textbooks, notebooks, and laptop are scattered across her quilt along with a pile of magazines and manicure stuff.

She clears a swath and flops down on her stomach. "Soooo. You and Max have a big date tonight?"

She obviously read his texts. What the hell? It's the first time she's mentioned him since she saw us together at the Corn Roast.

"He had to cancel, so I went to the Monday Night Movie Fest with Franklin," I explain.

"Oooh, smart move! Make Max jealous so he'll think twice before bailing on you with a phony excuse."

"That is *not* what I—and that's *not* what he—"

"You'd better watch out for Franklin, though. I don't think he's gotten any in a really long time. Maybe ever."

"*Devon!*"

She grins. "You're so touchy! Seriously, I was kidding. So things are going well with Max?"

"I thought you didn't want me hanging out with him," I say suspiciously.

She shrugs. "Yeah, well, I still think you're making a mistake. But if you insist on falling in love with Mr. Rich, Gorgeous, and Emotionally Unavailable . . . well, I'm here for you. You need all the help you can get. You're such a virgin, and I don't just mean sexually."

"*Excuse* me?" What is up with her tonight?

"God, it's not even fun to tease you anymore. You're too easy."

"Whatever." I slip off my shoes and lean back against the pillows. I read Max's other texts:

Did you get my message?

I told Franklin to find you. I'll call you tomorrow.

I exhale with relief. Max wasn't trying to weasel out of our date. Not that I was actually worried. It'll be so nice to spend some time with him tomorrow, even if it is just on the phone. Or if he's feeling better, maybe I can convince him to meet up for coffee.

"Hey. Speaking of upgrades?" Devon says.

"What?"

"I notice you don't have a laptop."

"Yeah, my old one broke, and I haven't had a chance to get a new one."

Which is a lie. The only computer I've ever owned is an ancient Dell desktop that's sitting in my room back home. It was a hand-me-down from Mom's brother Bud and has faded Yankees and NASCAR stickers all over it. There was a porno on the hard drive when I first got it, and Mom yelled at him for about six months for that.

"I have an extra, if you want to borrow it," Devon offers.

"You have an extra laptop?"

"Yeah. It's buried in my closet somewhere. I can dig it out and charge it for you tonight."

"Wow, thanks!" Maybe Devon likes me again.

"It was Becca's, actually."

I tense. "Oh."

"Her parents didn't want it. You might as well use it."

I'm not sure I want Becca's computer. That seems kind of creepy. "I don't know. Maybe it has sentimental value for you," I hedge.

"Don't be an idiot. It's just a piece of machinery. I only kept it as a backup in case mine was ever on the fritz." Devon sighs and opens her Spanish textbook. "You are so clueless sometimes."

"Sorry." I flush. I seem to be saying that a lot tonight. How is it that *she's* the bitchy one and I end up apologizing?

Still, Devon's right. I shouldn't make a big deal about Becca's computer. There's probably nothing personal stored on it, anyway. I'm sure her parents erased or transferred Becca's files after she died.

My phone beeps.

"Popular girl," Devon says sarcastically.

"Ha-ha."

It's a new text from an unfamiliar sender:

Lunch Thursday? K.

Killian? How did he get my number?

"Hey, Devon?"

"Hmm?"

"You know that guy Killian? The one who threw the party? What's his story, anyway?"

"Why?"

"I met him tonight."

Devon looks up from her textbook. "And what did you think?"

"He's, um . . . nice. And cute, I guess."

"If by 'cute' you mean Abercrombie model, then yeah. It runs in the family."

"Why? Who's he related to?"

"Killian didn't tell you?" she says, surprised. "He's Becca's cousin."

19.

On Tuesday morning before breakfast, I head to the third-floor Kerrith lounge to try out my new computer. Okay, so it's not mine, exactly, but having a sleek pink laptop, even a borrowed one, makes me feel more like a legitimate Thorn Abbey student. Plus now I can cyber-stalk people in private. For one thing, I want to Google Killian, now that I know he's Becca's cousin. Maybe I can figure out what's up between him and Max. And between him and Franklin, too, for that matter. It's the only way I'll get any information since I'm not allowed to talk to these people about each other.

The lounge is empty at this early hour. Devon and the girls have really spruced up the place. Before, it was a couple of old couches, a scratched-up coffee table, a small, boxy television set, and a metal bookshelf full of board games. The couches have been replaced with cushy new ones, and there's a small flat-screen TV.

A bunch of framed posters are propped up against the wall waiting to be hung. The top one is that famous painting of Shakespeare's Ophelia clutching a red poppy in her hand as she drowns. Which is a pretty weird choice, considering.

I lean back on one of the couches and boot up the laptop.

I flinch when the screen flashes to life.

The wallpaper is a photo of Max and Becca kissing on a dock. Behind them is a white sailboat. Its name is painted on the hull in shiny black letters: *Je Reviens.*

I gnaw on my thumbnail furiously. I *so* don't want to see this.

I start to change the wallpaper. But before I can go into the System Preferences section, I notice a single folder icon at the edge of the screen. RRW FILES.

RRW. Rebecca Rose Winters. Her parents didn't clean her computer after all. I start to click on the folder, then stop. Becca's files are none of my business. Instead, I click on the Safari icon and Google *"Je reviens."* It means "I return" in French.

Was that the boat Becca was sailing when she had her accident? I wonder. I Google her name along with the name of the boat, but nothing comes up.

I take a deep breath. Time to move on. Dwelling on Becca and Max's tragic love story will only put me in a foul mood.

Killian. Back to Killian.

I quickly pull up an article about Killian's mother, Jean Montgomery, and her sister Jane Winters, Becca's mother, co-chairing a fund-raiser for international adoption. There is another article about the two sisters that mentions how the Montgomery family splits their time between Philadelphia and London. That explains Killian's British accent.

I continue clicking. I come across an article about a party at the Metropolitan Museum of Art in New York City. There's a photo of Killian and Becca. *God, her again.* They are standing arm in arm in front of a massive bouquet of white roses. She is in a pale blue evening gown; he is in a black tux; they look like something out of a *Vogue* photo shoot. They are hanging out with half a dozen other teens—also dressed up, also magazine beautiful.

I linger on the image of Becca. Why does she have to be so insanely attractive?

The familiar fog of jealousy has started to seep into my brain. I go back to the desktop, to the folder labeled RRW FILES. Taking a deep breath, I click on it. I know I shouldn't, but I can't help it.

It's empty.

I gnaw at my thumbnail until it bleeds. The clock on the screen says that it's 8:50 a.m. I need to stop what I'm doing if I'm going to make it to philosophy on time.

But I can't. Stop, that is.

I start jabbing random keys, as though I could actually make Becca's files materialize out of thin air. Still nothing. This is nuts. What is wrong with me?

A drop of blood trickles from my thumb and smears on the touch pad. Enough. I slam the laptop shut and rise to my feet.

As I'm leaving the lounge, I hear the TV power on behind me. There is clapping and cheering, then static.

My heart pounding, I turn and scan the room slowly.

It's empty. Of course it's empty. I'm the only one here.

The static grows fainter as my ears start ringing with panic. I stride to the coffee table and reach for the remote as the room goes silent. The TV's dark. It's off.

A girl stares back at me from the screen, smirking.

It's not me. It's not my reflection.

I run.

20.

"WHAT'S WRONG?" MAX ASKS. HE REACHES ACROSS THE TABLE and laces his fingers with mine.

"Nothing." I force myself to smile and busy myself with my Coke. It's Friday night, and Max and I are having dinner together in a cozy restaurant in town called Le Canard Danse. I think it has something to do with a dancing duck, based on the sign outside, not on my nonexistent knowledge of French.

"Is it the food? I can get you something else."

"No, this is great. I love beef *à la bour . . . bourgi . . .* this dish." I fork a chunk of meat and pop it into my mouth. It's actually pretty delicious, even though it's unpronounceable. Fortunately, Max ordered for both of us.

I've been looking forward to having some quiet time with

Max, especially with all the strange stuff that's been happening lately. But I can't shake this stupid, insecure mood I'm in. Ever since we walked into the restaurant, it was obvious that Max has been here before. With Becca? The maître d' welcomed him with a "Nice to see you again, sir," and he gave me this funny look, as though he expected to see someone else on Max's arm: someone prettier, more glamorous, better dressed. Max knew what he wanted to order without even looking at the menu—steak and skinny little french fries, which he called "freets" or something—like he always orders the same thing.

But I can't ask Max if he used to come here with Becca because he'd think I was one of those needy, clingy girls.

And I can't tell him that I had a brief psychotic breakdown, searching for Becca's invisible files on her old laptop.

And I can't tell him that I met Becca's cousin Killian on Monday. Or that he invited me to lunch and that I had to make up an excuse to get out of it. Even though part of me was kind of tempted to go, if for no other reason than to get gossip about Max and Becca. And Franklin, too.

What are Max and I supposed to talk about when there are so many things I can't tell him?

"So are your mom and dad coming next weekend?" Max asks me.

"What? What's next weekend?"

"It's Parents' Weekend. You didn't get the five million e-mails from Dean Sanchez?"

"Oh. Yeah, that." I twist my napkin in my lap. How do I explain to a US senator's grandson that my mom just started a second job, at Applebee's, to make ends meet? Or that my dad isn't exactly around? Great, more things I can't tell him. "I don't think they can make it. They have, uh, other commitments they can't get out of. What about your parents?"

Max takes a sip of his water. "Yeah, they always show up for this stuff. They want to meet you."

"Really?" I ask, surprised.

"I mentioned you to my mom when we were Skyping the other day. She said she and Dad want to have dinner with us. Franklin, too," Max adds. "They like taking my friends out. I hope it's okay."

Maybe Devon was exaggerating. Mr. and Mrs. De Villiers don't sound "intimidating." They sound like nice, generous people. "Sure. That would be fun."

"Great." Max squeezes my hand. He seems sincerely happy that I'm meeting his parents. Which makes me happy. It's like we're a real couple.

"So what should I wear?" I ask him.

Max laughs. "What you always wear?"

"It's your parents. I want to make a good first impression."

"You'll be fine."

"I don't know." I've never met a boy's parents before, at least not the parents of a boy I was dating. Maybe Devon can give me some advice. Or better yet, let me borrow one of her outfits, as long as it's not the Las Vegas call girl dress.

"Seriously, just wear that." Max nods at my red sweater and denim skirt. "So did you finish your paper for Bags yet?"

Good. New topic. Talking about my wardrobe is stressful. "Almost. I'm having total writer's block with the ending."

"Me too. With the beginning, middle, *and* ending. I'm going to have to spend most of this weekend working on it to finish for Monday."

I guess that means I won't see him again till then. I bite back my disappointment. "Oh."

"I'll get it done. And if I don't . . . well, Bags is pretty cool about extensions."

"My friend Kayleigh swears she has this cure for writer's block," I say, trying to be helpful. "An hour on a treadmill, followed by a peanut butter and pickle sandwich, followed by a really strong cup of coffee. I've tried it, but it just gives me a stomachache."

Max smiles. "That would give me a stomachache, too."

The waiter comes by to fill our water glasses. A few tables

over, this girl I recognize from Kerrith—Taylor, Tabor?—is having dinner with a boy from my bio class. She laughs at something he says and touches his arm. He grins with pleasure, like a
happy, well-fed cat. How does she know how to do that? Is flirting a learnable skill? I have no idea how to talk to boys provoca-
tively or make those small but meaningful gestures. Other girls
make it look so easy, but it's like a foreign language to me. I'm
much more comfortable babbling about dumb stuff like peanut
butter and pickle sandwiches or sitting in a contented mutual
silence. It's funny, but Max seems to appreciate that.

Or does he? Maybe he's wondering why I'm not giggling
and touching his arm. Why I'm not more charming and
chatty, like Becca undoubtedly was, given that she was so
popular and the president of everything. What did the two
of them talk about? Probably smart, sophisticated things
like politics and art and music. Or fabulous places they'd
both been to.

Or maybe they just stared into each other's eyes, whispering about what they would do later in bed . . . in my bed.

"Tess? Do you want to order some dessert?" Max asks me.
The waiter hovers nearby with a couple of menus.

"Dessert? Sure."

Maybe more calories will help me get over my crazy jealousy.

⚜ ⚜ ⚜

When I get back to our room, Devon isn't there. It's late and I'm tired, and I have to get up early to finish my paper for Mr. Bagley.

I should go to sleep, but I'm feeling on edge. Depressed, even. My date with Max was fine, and he held my hand a lot. But he didn't kiss me good-bye in front of Kerrith. For a second he looked as though he might, but it was like he changed his mind at the last minute, saying, "Night, Tess," in a subdued voice.

Am I unkissable?

Or was he just missing Becca and wishing he was with her instead of me?

I grab the laptop, plop down on my bed, and boot up. At least I have my own wallpaper now: a picture of Marshmallow Fluff belly-up on my bed at home. Much better than Max and Becca making out by the beach.

I go online. There are three e-mails in my in-box. The first is from Dean Sanchez, with details about Parents' Weekend. The second is from my mom:

Hey, honey bunny!

Just wanted to let you know that I miss you and hope you are doing all right. I haven't heard from you lately, but I figure you must be busy with your classes and all.

Last week, I started my new waitressing job. It's been a while since I worked at a restaurant. I'd forgotten how annoying customers can be! One guy ordered a hamburger, but when I brought it to him, he claimed he'd ordered steak instead. He yelled at me for five minutes before asking to speak to the manager. I think he was just angling for a free steak!

By the way, I got a notice from your school about Parents' Weekend. I wish so much I could be there. I asked my boss for the time off, but he said there was no way since two of his other waitresses were on vacation then. Next year, I promise!

I hope you know how proud I am of you, being at that school. You are going to be a star someday.

Let me know if you need anything.

Hugs and kisses,

Mom

I feel so guilty. With everything that's been happening, I've forgotten all about my mom. I make a mental note to call her over the weekend so we can catch up. Of course, I'll have to leave out some details about the bonfire and Devon. Being a mom, she would worry way too much.

The second e-mail is from Kayleigh:

Hey, girl! ☺

Okay, so I've been living on Wikipedia and a bunch of other sites, trying to solve your mystery. I'm 99 percent sure there are supernatural forces at work. You should be super-careful!

Did you get an amulet yet? If not, order one ASAP. After you get it, NEVER TAKE IT OFF. It will protect you from Evil Spirits.

My fingers are stiff as I start to reply to Kayleigh. The room feels colder than it was a few minutes ago. *Way* colder. I wrap my comforter around my shoulders. Why is our radiator always breaking?

Hey, K! Thanks for the info. I feel like such a selfish friend. When we talked on Monday, I didn't even ask you how you are.

So, how are you? How are things with your parents? How's school?

It's been weird here, and I've been in this funk. I don't know what's wrong with me. I met this amazing guy, and

There is a loud scraping sound from Devon's side of the room. Startled, I glance up from the laptop. Devon's bottom desk drawer is open. I'm pretty sure it wasn't like that when I came in.

What the hell? Did it come loose on its own, or is a small animal trapped in there or something? Is Devon playing a prank on me?

I get up and walk over to the desk tentatively.

No small animals. The drawer is empty except for Devon's silver box. The one with Becca's photograph in it.

I kneel down for a closer look. The box has a beautiful flower design on it. Roses. I wonder if it holds other Becca mementos?

I try the lid. It doesn't budge. A warm tingling radiates up my fingers. It's the strangest sensation.

What is happening?

Footsteps, voices. I hear Devon shout, "Tell it to someone who cares, bitch!" and break into a peal of laughter. I close the drawer and retreat quickly to my bed.

I shut my laptop. I'll finish my e-mail to Kayleigh later. My brain is racing and spinning. It's crazy, but I feel as though the silver box beckoned, inviting me to open it.

Maybe Kayleigh is right after all. Maybe Thorn Abbey *is* haunted.

21.

"I THINK SHE SHOULD GO WITH AN LBD," YOONIE SUGGESTS. "You can't go wrong with an LBD."

"For her very first dinner with the parents? I don't think so, sweetie," Priscilla says. "Maybe in that slutty city you come from, but not here in the land of the Puritans. I think she should wear a Prada skirt, white blouse, and pearls."

Elinor pipes up. "I think you're both wrong. I'd go casual but elegant, like slacks and a cashmere sweater. And a sleek little Cartier watch."

It's Parents' Weekend, and in about an hour I'm meeting Max and his parents at a restaurant called the Hawk and Dove. Franklin will be there, too. I'm secretly relieved since the De Villierses won't be able to center the conversation on me.

Devon and her crew are giving me a makeover. Or, as Devon so sweetly put it, a "do-over." It's really nice of the girls to help me out. I wasn't sure they liked me before, especially Elinor and Priscilla. And Devon, half the time.

I perch on my bed in my bra and panties, with a thick layer of cold, muddy goop on my face that smells like cucumbers and dead leaves. Yoonie is straightening my hair with a long, hot metal thing. Priscilla is painting my fingernails pink, while Elinor puts the final touches on my pedicure.

Devon wipes the goop off my face with a wet washcloth. "I'm with Yoonie. We can add pearls for a touch of class. Tess, what do you have in the way of an LBD?"

"Um . . ." I have no idea what an LBD is. It sounds like a medical procedure.

"Actually, why am I asking you? I've seen your closet," Devon says impatiently. "It's like some Omaha, Nebraska, garage sale. Do you even own a little black dress?"

Versus a *big* black dress? And what's up with the bitchy garage sale comment? "No."

"You can borrow one of ours, then. The only problem is gonna be squeezing you in since you're practically a plus size." Devon bends over me with a pair of tweezers and yanks a hair from my right eyebrow.

"*Ow!* Do you *have* to do that?"

"This is for your own good. You look like a hobbit. Haven't you ever heard of waxing?"

"Devon, be nice," Priscilla chides her. "Tess is terrified enough as it is."

I turn toward Priscilla, or more like half-turn, since Yoonie's metal device is clamped to my hair like a pit bull's jaw. "Terrified? Why should I be terrified?"

"You know, sweetie. Meeting the De Villierses and all. Especially since—"

Devon shoots her a look of death. Priscilla falls silent and busies herself with a bottle of nail polish remover. What are they talking about? Do they mean because of Becca? Were Max's parents madly in love with her too?

"We're wasting time, people. We'll improvise." Devon strides over to her dresser. "Priscilla, you have that black silk skirt. It might fit her if we use some safety pins to let out the waist. Elinor, you can donate your black blouse with the ruffly collar; it's pretty baggy. Yoonie, you're a size eight shoe, right? We'll need your black flats, please. I'll throw in my pearls."

"I'm a size eight *narrow*," Yoonie clarifies. "But we can stretch them with this supercool hair dryer trick I know. Do you want the Miu Mius? Or the Marc Jacobs?" she asks me cheerfully.

"Um, either is fine, thanks."

"The Marc Jacobs, duh," Devon says. "Okay, let's move it! She has to be out of here in like thirty, forty minutes, tops. And we haven't even started on makeup, which is going to take forever."

This do-over isn't exactly helping my self-esteem.

At five thirty, Devon and I are alone in the room, putting the finishing touches on my outfit for dinner. Yoonie, Priscilla, and Elinor left to meet up with their own parents.

Devon drapes her string of pearls around my neck and snaps the clasp shut. "This necklace is vintage Mikimoto. If you lose it, I will seriously kill you." She spins me around. "There, what do you think?"

I stare at my reflection in the mirror. I look . . . pretty. And stylish. And put together. Not like me at all.

"Thank you, thank you, thank you!" I gush. "Wow, I wish I could look like this all the time."

"Yeah, dream on." Devon steps back and scrutinizes me with a frown.

"What is it?"

"I don't know. Something's missing." She glances over her shoulder at her closet.

"No, I'm fine. I'm better than fine. Besides, I have to go— and so do you. Aren't your parents waiting for you?"

"Nah. They're not coming this weekend. They can't stand being within ten feet of each other without their divorce lawyers present."

"I'm sorry."

"No biggie. I have other plans. Here, I have an idea. Just two more minutes, okay?"

She reaches into her makeup box and pulls out more tubes and jars. I close my eyes and try to quell my impatience as she draws on my lids with something wet. I feel her applying more lipstick, fussing with my hair, adjusting my blouse, and then . . .

"Perfection!" she exclaims. "What do you think?"

I open my eyes. "Devon!" I gasp. "I look like a—"

"Hottie? Yeah, you're welcome."

My lips are dark red, my eyes are lined with thick black eyeliner, and my hair is rumpled in a style that Kayleigh refers to as the "just got out of bed after a long night of you-know-what" look. Devon has also unbuttoned the top two buttons of my blouse so that a sliver of my bra peeks through.

I reach up to rebutton. "Devon, I can't!"

Devon grabs my hand. "You can't what? Handle *not* looking like a closet lesbian who shops at Walmart? Come on, Tess. Max will be all over you when he sees you."

I blush furiously. "I—I don't think so."

"Why not?"

"Because we're not like that."

Devon stares at me. "You two *have* done it, right?"

"Devon! We haven't even—" I start to bite my thumbnail, then stop.

"Made out with your clothes off?"

I shake my head.

"With your clothes *on*?"

I shake my head again.

"He hasn't even *kissed* you yet?" she says incredulously. "Oh my God. This is bad. Wow. Maybe he's decided he's gay."

"What?"

"I'm joking, you idiot. From everything Becca told me, he's . . . never mind. Anyway, this last-minute adjustment is totally fortuitous. Tonight's the night. If he doesn't stick his tongue down your throat when he sees you, we're going to have to take more drastic measures."

None of this conversation makes me feel better. *At all.*

22.

I FINALLY GET TO THE HAWK AND DOVE AT TEN AFTER SIX. FOR some reason, I thought the place would be chandeliers and frilly tablecloths and big, puffy flower arrangements. Instead, it's almost grim in its simplicity. The decor consists of stone-colored walls, wide-planked floors, and a deer's head mounted over an ancient brick fireplace.

I follow the stiff-backed maître d' to the De Villierses' table, a stupid grin frozen on my face. And limping, because Yoonie's Marc-whatever shoes are way too small, even with her hair dryer trick. I really don't want to meet Mr. and Mrs. De Villiers looking like this. I wish I could sneak into the ladies' room and undo my do-over. Or pretend to get an emergency call from my mom, someone, anyone, and simply bail.

When we reach the De Villierses' table, Max stands to greet me. He's in his dress uniform: navy blazer, white button-down shirt, khakis, and school tie.

"Tess," he says. "You're . . ." His eyes grow enormous as he takes in my face, my hair. "Ahh . . ." His gaze falls to the low, low neckline of my blouse. "Yeah, so, these are my parents. Mom, Dad, this is my friend Tess Szekeres."

Mr. De Villiers and Franklin both stand too. Franklin is also in his dress uniform. "Tess," Mr. De Villiers says, extending his hand. "Very nice to meet you."

Mrs. De Villiers doesn't offer me her hand but gives me a tight-lipped smile. She has this terrifying way of communicating complete and total disapproval without uttering a single word.

Franklin shoots me a sympathetic look.

Oh, God, this is already a disaster. Of epic proportions.

The maître d' hovers beside me. Why is he still there? Then I realize he wants me to sit. I twist my body awkwardly and sink down onto my chair at the same moment that he slides it out. It's like a bad screwball comedy, and I almost fall to the floor.

The maître d' grabs my arm to steady me. "Pardon me!" he says, sounding mortified.

"Are you okay?" Franklin asks.

"I'm fine. I'm such a klutz!" I scramble onto my seat and

quickly adjust my skirt to hide the safety pins. "I hope I haven't kept you all waiting!" I say a little too loudly.

"We just got here," Max says in a tense voice.

"What can we get you to drink, Tess?" Mr. De Villiers asks me jovially.

"A Coke, please."

"A Coke for the young lady!"

The maître d' bows and slips away.

I take a second to compose myself and check out Max's parents. Mr. De Villiers looks like an older version of Max, with ruddy cheeks and thinning hair and a big linebacker's build. Mrs. De Villiers is slim and regal and beautiful, with glossy, shoulder-length auburn hair and flawless, dewy skin.

I notice that she's wearing gray slacks and a matching cashmere cardigan. Her only accessories are her wedding rings, a small diamond pendant, and a thin silver watch that I swear says "Cartier."

I should have listened to Elinor and gone with the pants and sweater.

I should *not* have listened to Devon about tweaking my outfit at the last minute. Or about anything whatsoever.

A waiter comes by with my Coke, which is in a crystal goblet filled with crushed ice. Mr. De Villiers hands him his own empty glass and says, "Talisker. Neat."

"Right away, sir."

I take advantage of the distraction and discreetly rebutton the top of my blouse. Mrs. De Villiers narrows her eyes at me and clears her throat.

"Lucia. You haven't touched your drink," Mr. De Villiers says.

"I don't care for this kind of vermouth," Mrs. De Villiers replies testily.

"Well, this nice young man will get you another one, then. With a different vermouth." He turns to me. "So, Tess! Max tells us you're new to Thorn Abbey."

"Yes, sir. I just started in September."

"Tess is a fantastic writer," Franklin pipes up. "Mr. Bagley asked her to read an excerpt from her *French Lieutenant's Woman* paper to the class on Wednesday. It blew the rest of our papers out of the water."

"Yeah, well, speak for yourself. I got an A-minus on mine," Max boasts.

"Yes, well, I got an A," Franklin banters back. "Tess is the only one who got an A-plus, though. She could teach us both a thing or two about modern literature."

"I was never a big fan of Mr. Fowles, myself," Mr. De Villiers says. "Now, Charles Dickens, he could spin a tale. I don't suppose you kids read him in any of your classes? 'It is a far, far better thing that I do, than I have ever done . . .'"

"It is a far, far better rest, that I go to, than I have ever known,'" I finish.

Mr. De Villiers beams at me. "A fellow Dickens aficionado. Wonderful!"

The waiter comes by with more drinks. Mrs. De Villiers takes a sip of her martini and says, "Better. So, Tess. Max tells us your parents weren't able to make it this weekend. Do they live very far away?"

Oh, God. The interrogation has begun. "Yes. I mean, no. My mom had to work tonight."

"Oh? And how about your father?"

"My dad? He doesn't live with us."

Max raises his eyebrows at me.

"So they're divorced?" Mrs. De Villiers persists.

I twist my napkin in my lap. "Not exactly."

Now everyone is staring at me. I must sound like an idiot. Mr. De Villiers leans over to his wife. "It's really not any of our business," he says softly.

"No, it's okay. The thing is, I don't know very much about him because they're not married. They were never married. He was my mom's high school boyfriend, and after I was born, we never really saw him again."

More silence. *So* awkward. I rush on, trying to fill it.

"He moves around a lot. I think he's living in New Mexico

now. Like in Albuquerque or Santa Fe. His parents—they're my grandparents, I guess—live in Albany, and my mom runs into them once in a while. They said he's working at a gas station or a garage or somewhere having to do with cars. And he's in a band, too. The Tequila Shooters, I think. . . ."

I hear myself babbling on and on, and I can't stop, although I wish I could. I watch Max and Franklin and the De Villierses watching me, pitying me, being freaked out by me, or maybe just trying to mentally erase me from their lives. I don't know why I picked this moment to blurt out my entire pathetic family history. I'm sure Max doesn't know, either. He looks more uncomfortable than I've ever seen him. Which is saying a lot.

And then, somehow, Franklin saves the day. "Yeah, my cousin Phoebe was raised by a single mom too. Yours sounds awesome, from everything you've told me, Tess." He turns to Mr. De Villiers. "And speaking of cars, sir, Max told me you just got a new Ferrari. Well, a new *old* Ferrari. 1956?"

"1957," Mr. De Villiers says proudly. "A 250 GT California Spyder LWB. I've been dreaming about this particular model since I was barely older than you boys. Previous owner lives just outside Boston. In fact, Lucia and I are going to make a little detour and pick it up on our way home on Sunday."

"*Must* we?" Mrs. De Villiers asks, scrunching up her face.

151

"I promised the Kennistons we'd attend their dinner party. It's at seven."

"Fine, you can drive back to the city without me. I'll take the train into Boston. Max, you want to come with me and see the car? You're welcome to join us too, Franklin," Mr. De Villiers says.

"I'll have to check my calendar. Coach might be adding an extra practice to prep for our match next week with Emerson," Max says.

"Same here, sir. But thank you for the invitation," Franklin adds.

The three of them continue talking about soccer games and vintage cars while Mrs. De Villiers quietly sips her drink. At one point, Franklin turns and smiles at me. I never told him a thing about my mom. But he just knew.

I mouth: *Thank you.*

Franklin mouths: *You're welcome.*

I take a deep breath, feeling calmer than I've felt all night.

Until I notice Max glaring at the two of us.

23.

THERE IS A BRIGHT FULL MOON IN THE SKY AS MAX WALKS ME
to Kerrith Hall. Which is good, since it gives me something to
focus on while I fight back tears and wait for him to dump me.

He hasn't said a word since we left the restaurant. His
parents went back to their hotel, and Franklin went back to
Chapin Hall. Mr. De Villiers gave me a hearty handshake and
wished me "all the best." Mrs. De Villiers said, "Nice to have
met you," in a past-tense way that implied there would be no
future dinners. And Franklin patted my arm and told me not
to forget about Marilyn and Tony on Monday. It took me a
minute to realize he was talking about the upcoming movie,
Some Like It Hot.

But from Max? Nothing. We just walked toward Kerrith

like we did after the Corn Roast and our date at the dancing duck restaurant, except not speaking at all.

We pass the stone fountain, the library, Lanyon. The quad is more crowded than usual, with students and parents wandering around like tourists. Max stuffs his hands into his pockets and gazes out at the distance. I fill the uncomfortable silence with my own inner chatter, replaying the evening like an awful, but mesmerizing, car accident: the do-over, the do-over of the do-over, hobbling into the restaurant in Yoonie's Cinderella shoes, practically falling on my butt at the De Villierses' table, Mrs. De Villiers's tidal wave of scorn and rejection, my failed Oprah moment as I spilled my broken-home sob story.

Mr. and Mrs. De Villiers are probably having their own postmortem recap session right this second: *What is Max thinking, dating a girl like that? Surely there's someone more appropriate for him at Thorn Abbey. More like Becca Winters . . .*

"Did I ever show you *The Eternal Spirit?*"

"I'm sorry. The what?" I'm so startled by Max's out-of-the-blue question that my voice comes out in a squeak.

"Come on."

Max takes my elbow and guides me off the main path, away from the busy quad. Pretty soon, we are alone on a narrow dirt trail that snakes behind Lanyon. We proceed single file. I don't remember this from Devon's unofficial tour.

The trail winds through a grove of hemlock trees. It's dark back here except for the thin gauze of moonlight that filters through the branches. Something stirs in the underbrush and skitters away into the night. I jump back and give a little yelp. Max doesn't seem to notice and plunges ahead, hands in his pockets, deep in thought.

And then, suddenly, we are in a small mossy clearing. With two old-fashioned gravestones. And a marble statue of a young woman.

I gasp. Becca is buried *here*?

But why are there *two* gravestones?

"Um, Max? W-what is this place?" I stammer nervously. I don't know why he would bring me here.

"This is where the Thorns are buried."

"The Thorns?"

"You know. Augustus Thorn and his wife, Aurora. Thorn Abbey used to be their private estate ages ago, before it was a school."

"Oh." Relief courses through me. Max didn't want to show me Becca's burial ground after all. That would have been beyond horrible and creepy.

Max points to the statue. "That's *The Eternal Spirit*. It's supposed to be Aurora. I guess she died when she was pretty young. He had it made in her honor by some famous sculptor."

I take a few tentative steps toward the statue. Aurora Thorn is beautiful, with wavy hair cascading down to her waist and an angelic face. She's wearing a long, lovely dress with a romantic, ruffly skirt and a rose tucked behind one ear. There is a ring of white rosebushes—real ones—planted around her feet.

The gravestone beside her is inscribed:

AURORA ELIZA THORN

1830-1858

Beloved wife

Flowers bloom and die

And bloom and die again.

Time may have taken you from me,

But our love is everlasting.

The gravestone next to hers is inscribed, simply:

AUGUSTUS FREDERICK THORN

1820-1879

I read the inscription on Aurora's grave again. My heart plummets. Max is obviously trying to tell me something— about everlasting love, about Becca.

"I know why you brought me here," I whisper.

"What?"

"You don't want to see me anymore. You're breaking up with me. And it's okay. We can go back to being friends. I mean, that is, if you want to. Or we can just pretend we don't even know each other."

Max frowns. "What in the hell are you talking about?"

"Look, I get it. You still have feelings for—" I suck in a deep breath and clasp my hands to keep them from shaking. "Besides, I don't fit into your world. I got that loud and clear tonight. Your mom hated me. Your dad probably hated me too. I'm never, ever going to be the kind of girl they want you to be with. The kind of girl *you* want to be with."

Max narrows his eyes at me. "Oh? What kind of girl do I want to be with?"

"The kind of girl who knows what to wear. Who knows how to act in fancy restaurants. Who doesn't make a complete fool of herself when she meets your parents for the first time."

"Are you *insane?*"

He grabs my wrist and pulls me toward him. We're standing so close that I can feel his breath on my face.

"Max, I—"

"Be quiet."

The next thing I know, his lips are on mine, pressing, probing. A million shooting stars are fizzing and popping in my

157

brain. My legs feel as though they're going to buckle out from under me. I've never been kissed like this. I will never be kissed like this again.

When we finally pull apart, we're both breathing hard.

"Okay?" he asks.

"Okay what?" I gasp.

"I brought you here because I wanted to be alone with you."

"Oh."

"Seriously, I don't know where you come up with these ideas about 'my world.' I like you *because* you don't know what to wear. Or how to act in fancy restaurants. And my parents make everyone nervous. Especially my mom. My dad's okay, but only after he's had a couple of drinks."

I'm still so dizzy from the kiss that I can barely process what he's saying. "But you looked so miserable tonight. Like you were mad at me," I manage.

"I wasn't mad at you. Being with my parents stresses me out, that's all. Plus you kind of caught me off guard with that outfit. It's not like you."

I run my hand across Priscilla's black skirt, feeling the bumps where the safety pins are. "Devon and the girls thought I should dress up. You know, since I was meeting your parents," I confess.

"Devon! I should have known." Max's face darkens. "If I

wanted to be with someone like her or her friends, I would. But I want to be with you. Do you understand?"

I stare at him in wonder. He wants to be with me. *Me.*

"For a really smart girl, you can be really dense," he says.

I grin. My heart is bursting with happiness. "Yeah, I know."

He cradles my face in his hand and kisses me again—this time more tenderly. A cold breeze comes up, and I nestle closer to him. He wraps his arms around me tightly. We stay like this for a long time, not moving.

Behind him, the statue of Aurora Thorn shimmers in the moonlight. And I finally relax. Max likes me for me. The dead are exactly that: dead. I don't have anything to be afraid of anymore.

24.

THE REST OF PARENTS' WEEKEND IS A WHIRLWIND OF TEAS, lectures, art shows, and concerts. It's late Sunday morning, and I'm in the Kerrith parlors at the farewell brunch. Everyone's parents seem to be there except for mine: Priscilla's mom and dad, who arrived Friday on their private jet; Elinor's, who drove up in a cream-colored Rolls-Royce with their three hyperactive whippets; and Yoonie's mom, who flew in from LA while her dad stayed at home with their four-year-old twins.

Even Devon's dad showed up unexpectedly yesterday. Except that she is beyond furious because he brought along his new girlfriend.

"They're not even effing *divorced* yet," Devon snipes under her breath.

She, Priscilla, Elinor, Yoonie, and I are standing at the buffet table. She picks up a blueberry scone and stuffs it into her mouth, crumbs flying everywhere. "And look at her. God, what is she, like twenty?"

We all turn. Devon's dad and his girlfriend are wandering around the room, sipping coffee, whispering to each other. The girlfriend is rail thin with enormous boobs and a short blond pixie cut. She's wearing rhinestone-studded jeans, a formfitting pink top, and stiletto heels.

"Nah, she's old. At least thirty. She's just had a lot of work done," Yoonie observes.

"Whatever. The only reason he brought her is because he knows I'll tell Mommy, and she'll totally lose it, and they'll scream at each other on the phone about this for the next two weeks," Devon says. "I swear, they only exist to make each other miserable. I wish they'd just kill each other and get it over with."

"Oh, honey. You want one of my Klonies?" Elinor suggests gently.

"God, yes!"

Elinor reaches into her purse and hands Devon a little yellow pill. "Swallow that down with your vodka and cranberry. You'll feel better right away."

"Thanks, El." Devon pops the pill into her mouth and takes

a big sip. I glance at my plastic cup, alarmed. I thought it was just juice.

"Shit! Now they're making out!" Devon whines.

We all turn again. Devon's dad and the girlfriend are indeed making out, next to the "local authors" bookshelf and the cracked bust of the poet Edna St. Vincent Millay. Nearby, Mrs. Frith glares at them over the top of her tiny wire-rimmed glasses, and a bunch of freshman girls stifle giggles.

Priscilla hooks her arm through Devon's. "I'm so sorry, sweetie. Why don't the five of us get out of here and get some fresh air?"

The five of us. Cool, I'm included.

"Yeah, okay." Devon sighs.

We forge a path through the crowded room and make our way out to the quad. It's a picture-perfect fall day: brilliant blue sky, glorious foliage, and crisp air that smells faintly of apples. In the distance, I can see the parking lot, cars, a few students hugging their parents good-bye.

For a moment, I think about my mom. I wish she could have been here.

I instinctively look around for Max, but he's nowhere in sight. I haven't seen him since Friday night. He texted me that he was busy keeping his mom and dad entertained, plus he has soccer practice this afternoon. We have a tentative date later tonight, though. We might go into town or just go for a walk. I can't wait.

Max. My heart beats a little faster at the thought of him. I still can't believe we're really together.

"Hey, you guys want to head down to the beach and get high?" Yoonie suggests.

"That is *the* best idea I've heard all weekend," Devon says.

"I just need to say bye to the parental unit. It'll take two seconds," Yoonie says.

"Ditto," Priscilla says.

Elinor nods. "Me too."

"Actually, um, I need to go to the library. I have a ton of homework to do," I say quickly.

Devon crosses her arms over her chest. "You've never gotten high before, have you?"

I think about the time Kayleigh and I smoked a joint. Well, she smoked it, and I watched her. When she passed it to me, I had a crazy coughing fit before I even put the joint in my mouth. That was the extent of it. "Of course I have," I fib. "I really do have a lot of homework, though. There's a big quiz in algebra, and I have like thirty pages to read for American history, and—"

"You are such a terrible liar. Are you and Max meeting up?" Devon asks.

I blush. "No! I mean, not right this second. He's got soccer."

"Ohmigod, Tess! You never told us. How was your big dinner with Mr. and Mrs. D.?" Priscilla asks me.

"She's kind of a bitch, right? But he's pretty chill," Yoonie says.

"I caught him checking out my ass once," Elinor says.

"What ass?" Devon points out. "In any case, our Tess isn't talking. I tried to beat the details out of her yesterday, but no success. But maybe the pot will loosen her tongue."

"Seriously, I can't," I plead. "I'll see you guys later, okay?"

I give a little wave and take off in the direction of the library. Behind me, I hear Elinor say, "What's wrong with her today?" and Devon's reply: "You mean, what's wrong with her, *period*. That girl is hopeless."

Whatever. I have Max now. I don't need Devon's approval—or the other girls' either.

Although Devon is right: I don't actually need to go to the library. But I really, really don't want to smoke pot with them. I also don't feel like going down to the beach. I've been avoiding it since that day I found Max on the cliff. Too many bad memories—for him, for me. I still get the chills, remembering how I came across him that morning on the ledge.

I figure I'll kill some time reading. Then I can double back to Kerrith and enjoy some peace and quiet.

As I pass the stone fountain, I notice Gita from Kerrith sitting on the bench with her parents. "This is Becca's fountain," I hear Gita say.

I stop in my tracks. *Becca's fountain?*

"That's what the students all call it, anyway," Gita adds.

"Becca is the sophomore who died last spring," Gita's mom reminds the dad. "Such a tragedy. She was a lovely girl. So full of promise."

"Oh, yes, I remember," the dad says. "It's very nice they have this memorial for her."

Gita notices me just then. She smiles nervously and waves— probably because she realizes I overheard her talking about my boyfriend's ex-girlfriend.

"Hey, Tess," she calls out. "I'm showing my parents around."

"That's nice," I reply stiffly.

Gita says something else, but I mutter an excuse and keep walking. I can't believe this fountain is a memorial to Becca. I can't believe no one told me.

I think about the time I followed Max out of the movie and found him throwing pebbles at the stone pillar. Does he like to sit by the fountain and think about her?

Now I'm in a *really* bad mood.

I reach the library and run up the steps two at a time. The lobby's almost empty, except for a man and a woman admiring some student photographs on the wall. The woman looks over, and I stop in my tracks and clamp my hand over my mouth to keep from screaming.

Becca.

No, not Becca. It's a woman who looks a lot like her. She has the same pale blond hair, which is pulled back into a ponytail; the same cheekbones; the same blue eyes. She's wearing an elegant black suit and high-heeled boots.

The man with her turns too. A young man. Killian Montgomery.

His face lights up. "Well, hello there, stranger!"

"Um . . . hi." I can't stop staring at the woman.

"Killian? Aren't you going to introduce me to your friend?" the woman prompts him.

"Oh, my apologies. Where are my manners? Tess, this is my mother, Jean Montgomery. Mother, this is my very dear friend Tess Szekeres."

Becca's aunt. "Hello, Mrs. Montgomery," I say, trying to recover my composure.

"Hello, Tess," Mrs. Montgomery says. "I don't remember Killian mentioning you."

"Tess and I have just recently become acquainted. You could say it was love at first sight. Isn't that right, Tess?" Killian walks over and wraps his arm around my shoulders.

"I, um."

"You've been ignoring me, you bad girl! Where have you been?"

"I'm sorry. I've been really busy," I say, flustered.

He tousles my hair playfully. "I am absolutely taking you to lunch. Next Saturday. And this time, I won't take no for an answer."

I'm not sure how to decline politely. "Um, okay."

"Then it's settled. And don't you dare try to cancel. I will march into Kerrith, throw you over my shoulder, and carry you to Le Canard Danse if I have to."

"Honestly, Killian," Mrs. Montgomery chides him.

"Just a figure of speech, Mother. You and I need to get to the airport or you'll miss your flight to Philly," Killian says, tapping his watch.

"Yes, of course. It was nice to meet you, Tess."

"It was nice to meet you too, Mrs. Montgomery."

Killian pecks me on the cheek, then escorts his mother out the door. I stand there as though I'd been sucker punched. Twice. First I learn about Becca's stupid fountain. Then I find out that Becca's aunt was here for Parents' Weekend. Did Max see her? Did they reminisce about Becca? Was he lying to me when he said he was busy with his parents and with soccer practice all weekend?

Jealousy and anxiety overwhelm me. I rub my throbbing temples. I almost wish I had gone down to the beach with Devon and the girls.

Of course, I could still go.

Instead, I head back to my room. I'm tired of all these secrets. And with Devon occupied, I'm finally going to get some answers.

25.

Kerrith Hall is silent as a grave. I guess everyone is still saying good-bye to their parents, or hanging out on the quad, or getting high on the beach, or whatever.

Up in the room, I quickly lock the door. I'm not sure how long I have until Devon gets back.

I want to get past my confusion, doubt, and insecurity once and for all. Becca's laptop is a blank slate, and I can't find anything useful online. Devon's silver box is the only place left that may hold clues to Becca and Max's relationship—and the tension between the people in their little orbit, like Killian and Franklin.

What is in that box? Besides that photo of Becca in her sexy bikini, that is?

I dig through Devon's jewelry chest. I find the key in a nest of necklaces and bracelets, then I hurry over to her desk and pull the box out of her bottom drawer.

I wait for the same warm, tingling sensation as before. Nothing. I run my hand over the entire surface. Still nothing. I wonder if I imagined the whole thing. Maybe it was static shock, like when you walk across carpet and touch metal?

It's not important now. Excited and nervous, I insert the key and lift the lid.

The box is filled to the brim with mementos. There are more photographs of Becca. Photographs of Becca and Devon. Airline ticket stubs for trips to Paris, London, Madrid. Dried flower petals. A white silk scarf. A teddy bear key chain. A tube of shimmery pink lipstick. An empty perfume bottle.

I touch the perfume bottle to my wrist and inhale deeply. The fragrance is so familiar, but I can't quite place it. I pick up the white silk scarf and wrap it around my neck. It is impossibly soft, like a whisper.

And then something catches my eye. Underneath the pile of keepsakes is a red leather diary. With the initial *B* emblazoned on the cover, in gold.

I lift the diary with trembling hands and open it to the first page. I recognize Becca's lovely, florid handwriting:

September 18

Today was a good day. It was so warm outside. D and
I skipped lunch and gave each other mani-pedis on
the lawn. Then I had <u>Streetcar</u> auditions after class.
Fingers crossed, but I think I might get the part of
Blanche. Mr. R was smiling at me during my 'kindness of
strangers' speech like I was Vivien Leigh reincarnated.
Or maybe he just enjoyed my outfit. Mother would so
not approve of the tight dress I wore to audition, but I
really want the part. (Ha!)

  After dinner, D and I watched old <u>Buffy</u> episodes
on her laptop and drank shots. I'm so glad she and
I are roommates again this year. She is the most loyal
friend I have ever had. I only wish I could talk to her
about M. Maybe one of these days I will.

  I frown. Why couldn't Becca tell Devon about Max? Were
they keeping their relationship under wraps in the beginning?
Or did Becca have a secret crush on him?
  I read on:

  Speaking of M, he texted tonight and said he wants
to meet up this weekend. I don't know what to tell him.

I want to be with him, but I know I shouldn't. I'm so mixed up.

Now *I'm* mixed up. Why couldn't Becca be with him? Unless by "be with" she meant something else . . . as in sex? I can relate to that, since all I've ever done with Max or any boy is kiss. It's weird and annoying, thinking that Becca and I share this problem.

Shared, I correct myself.

I skip ahead several pages:

September 24

D and I went skinny-dipping at the beach yesterday. The water was cold but not freezing. I thought we were alone, but I spotted Mr. S on top of the cliff, watching us. As soon as he saw me notice him, he left. Creeper.

M sailed by at one point in the boat, and D and I gave him a peek. Bad girls! ☺

Last night, D spent the night down the hall, and M spent the night in our room. Heaven.

My stomach twists. Okay, so I guess they did have sex after all. I imagine Max watching Becca's beautiful, naked body jumping in the waves, and Devon's, too. I imagine Max and Becca alone, later. . . .

I really don't want to read any more. But I can't help myself. I flip to a random page in the middle.

January 14

I'm so miserable. I want to die.

Wait, what? Why was she miserable? Becca was supersuccessful and popular. She and Max were in love. They were having hot sex.

This doesn't make any sense.

In the hallway, voices and footsteps approach. I scramble to put Becca's diary back in the box just as I found it and unravel her scarf from my neck. I lock everything up and put the key back. The voices and footsteps grow louder, then recede.

I stare at Devon's desk drawer, breathing hard. I can still smell Becca's perfume on my skin.

Becca was—is—the enemy. But now she's more than that; she's a mystery.

Who was the real Becca? The perfect girl with the perfect life? Or a girl with dark secrets? Or both?

❧ ❧ ❧

I am walking down the path, the one that winds through the woods by Thorn Abbey and leads down to the beach. The air is cool and wet with rain, and my footsteps are light on the carpet of brown fallen leaves as I hurry down to the place where I know he is waiting for me. My cheeks are cold, and my heavy wool sweater scratches against my skin, but I don't care, because I can already feel his strong arms around my body and his warm lips against mine.

And then I am at the bottom of the hill. The beach rises above the horizon, endless and gray. Suddenly I feel exposed. Frightened. The air is different here: bigger, less forgiving. It smells like the sea and salt and dead things.

I move closer to the water. A wave rushes up to my boots and then snakes away, leaving two identical dark stains. I shudder against the chill and look around. Where is he, and why is he late?

I wake with a start. The room is frigid. The window is open, and the curtains are flapping and twisting in the breeze. Across the room, Devon's bed is empty. The clock reads 6:20 a.m. Where is she?

Still dazed from my dream, I get up to close the window. That's when I see the words scrawled in big, drippy red letters on the wall above my bed:

BE CAREFUL

26.

"IT WASN'T THERE WHEN I WENT TO BED LAST NIGHT," I INSIST.

The security guard, whose name tag reads ALFRED, peers skeptically at the message on the wall. He leans over and sniffs. "Cherries," he pronounces.

"Excuse me?"

"Cherries. That lip stuff you gals wear," he says.

I lean over and sniff too. He's right: It smells like fruity lip gloss.

"I'm guessing your roommate decided to play a prank on you," Alfred says. "Did you ask her?"

Devon's bed is still made up. She never came home last night. But I can't tell Alfred that or he might report her to Mrs. Frith for missing curfew.

"Um, she's taking a shower," I fib. "She didn't write that, though. I asked her."

"This isn't the sort of thing most people'll admit to, if you know what I mean," Alfred points out. "You two fighting over a fellow?"

"No!" *But sometimes, it feels as though her ex-roommate and I are.*

"Look, I'll make a note of it. Let me know if it happens again."

"I will. Thank you."

Alfred leaves. I glance at my clock. It's just after seven a.m. I wonder if Alfred is right—or half right, anyway? Did I forget to lock the door before I went to bed? Maybe some freaky Kerrith girl snuck into the room in the middle of the night and scribbled that message on my wall?

But why? And be careful of what?

It's scary to think it happened while I was sleeping, even if it *was* a dumb, innocent prank.

I consider calling Max to tell him about the incident. Girls call their boyfriends about stuff like this, right? I'm not sure what he would say or do, though. Maybe he'd think it was a prank too, and that I was overreacting.

Last night, he and I went for a walk after dinner, and I felt the old distance creeping between us. He was moody, like something was weighing on him. I wanted to tell him

I know about "Becca's fountain." I also wanted to tell him that I'd met Becca's aunt and to ask him if he'd seen her this weekend too.

But I couldn't bring myself to do it. I didn't want to seem paranoid or jealous, even though that's how I was feeling inside.

I also wanted to tell him about the silver box. But that was out of the question too. *Oh, yeah, by the way, I broke into Devon's stuff and started reading your ex-girlfriend's diary. She wrote these things about you that didn't make any sense. . . .*

Max and I were so close on Friday, when he kissed me and told me how he felt about me. I wish we could go back to that.

I wish there were no secrets between us.

I grab a sweatshirt and start scrubbing at the message on the wall.

I wish I knew what the hell was going on.

At lunch, Devon and Yoonie show up fifteen minutes later than usual and plunk their trays down on the table. They're both pale, and their eyes are bloodshot.

Devon frowns at her salad. "Ugh. There's no way I can eat this."

"Me neither. Maybe we should fast today. You know, restore our purity and equilibrium," Yoonie suggests.

"Yes! Smart! Tess, what *is* that? It smells disgusting."

"It's a tuna sandwich," I say defensively. "Are you guys all right?"

"We overindulged yesterday," Yoonie explains delicately.

What am I supposed to say to that? "I'm sorry. Where are Priscilla and Elinor?"

"They're still asleep. I crashed with them." Devon eyes my food. "You don't need this." She picks up my tray and hands it to a nearby cafeteria lady. "Take this away, please."

"Devon! I was eating that!"

"Seriously, don't make me lecture you about calories again. That stuff's loaded with mayo. And did you forget about carbs?" Devon pushes her own tray aside. "So what did you do yesterday after you bailed on us? Hot date with the boyfriend?"

"I went to the library. Then Max and I went for a walk after dinner."

"Wow, you're like an old married couple." Devon smirks.

"Here." Yoonie slides her salad over to me. "*I* think you and Max are super-cute together."

"Thanks, Yoonie. And thanks for the salad," I say.

"No probs."

Of the four girls, Yoonie has always been the nicest to me. Followed by Priscilla, followed by Elinor. Devon is a total wild card. One minute she is kind and protective of me, like a big sister. The next minute, she reduces me to emotional rubble. And seems to enjoy it.

Devon digs through her purse and slips on a pair of bronze-colored sunglasses. "It's obvious why you and Max are together, isn't it?" she remarks. "You're a rebound. A safe choice. Max doesn't want to risk getting emotionally involved after what happened."

She's obviously in emotional-rubble mode. "Excuse me?"

"Sorry, that came out wrong. What I meant was, you're a really, really nice person. And I'm sure Max feels really, really comfortable with you," Devon says sweetly.

I grit my teeth, wishing I could think of a good comeback. The problem is . . . what if Devon is right?

27.

"IT'S NICE TO SEE YOU AGAIN, MISS," SAYS THE MAÎTRE D' AT
Le Canard Danse. "You too, sir," he adds to Killian.

Killian turns to me. "So you've been here before. No doubt
with old Maxi. I'm terribly jealous."

I blush and stammer and explain about having dinner here
with Max a couple of weekends ago. The maître d' leads us to
our table. I remember to let him pull out my chair, and I sit
down semi-gracefully. I learned my lesson at the Hawk and
Dove.

The waiter comes by to take our drink orders. He's the same
one who served Max and me. "We have the *boeuf bourguignon*
on the lunch menu today," he tells me helpfully. "But if you'd
prefer something lighter, we have some lovely fish specials."

"No, the beef is great," I say immediately.

"My, what a sophisticated palate you have," Killian compliments me. "I'll have the same. And we'll share the cheese plate after."

"Very good, sir."

The waiter disappears. Killian steeples his hands under his chin and smiles affably at me. "So, here we are. I'm so glad I lured you away from your very busy schedule."

I hesitate. I can't exactly tell Killian that I've been avoiding him after Franklin's warning.

"There's so much homework at this school," I say lightly. "I feel like I practically live at the library!"

"You're one of those responsible, studious types. How charming," Killian says. "I myself have a very efficient system: I do the minimum work necessary to maintain a B average. That gives me the freedom I require to pursue other interests."

"Like?" I ask curiously.

"Oh, this and that. Lacrosse. Sailing. Throwing soirees. Helping my uncle manage a hedge fund."

The word "uncle" jolts me—Becca's father? I probably shouldn't plunge right into the million questions I have about her. "What's a hedge fund?" I ask instead.

"That's the problem with these uppish private schools like Thorn Abbey. They don't teach us anything practical. A hedge fund is an investment vehicle for people who have a lot of money and aren't afraid to play with it."

"That sounds interesting. Is that what you want to do someday? For a career, I mean?" I find myself oddly comfortable talking to Killian and asking him questions about himself. There is an easy air about him, like we're two old friends sitting around and catching up.

"I have no idea. If I had my druthers, I'd rather not have to pin myself down to something as tedious as a *career*." He grins. "But enough about me. What about you? What do you do for kicks, darling? Besides while away the hours with your high-maintenance boyfriend, that is?"

"High maintenance?" I repeat. What is he talking about? And how would he know what kind of boyfriend Max is?

"You are loyal to the bone, aren't you? You don't need to pretend with me. Becky used to tell me all about his mood swings. One minute, a ray of sunshine. The next minute, a veritable typhoon. Of course, it was nothing that a good psychiatrist and twenty milligrams of Prozac a day couldn't cure."

"B-Becky?"

"Yes, my cousin. I thought you knew?"

"I thought her name was Becca."

"That's what everyone called her. She and I had our own nicknames for each other. We grew up in the same neighborhood in Philly. Chestnut Hill. We were in diapers and pre-school and all that nonsense together." He smiles sadly. "She died, you know."

"Yes. I'm so sorry."

The waiter comes by to fill our water glasses, then moves on to a young couple at the next table. I'm glad Killian brought up Becca. I really want to learn more about her from some-one who was obviously very close to her. But I don't want to intrude on his grief. He seems so melancholy suddenly.

"You know how it happened, don't you?" he asks.

"Sort of. Not really. She was sailing, right?"

"Yes. She loved to sail." Killian closes his eyes. "One night last May, she took one of the school's boats out to sea, without permission. A little Sunfish. A bad storm came up, and the boat washed ashore without her."

"That's so awful." I knew she died in a sailing accident from the newspaper article. I didn't know these details, though. "Was she alone?"

"Apparently. They didn't find her body for weeks." Killian opens his eyes and stares at me. "Poor old Maxi blames himself for her death, I think."

"What? Why?" I gasp. This was the last thing I expected to hear.

"He told the police the two of them had been out on a

date and they had a little spat. She took off, and he didn't go after her. That's when she must have gone down to Whitwater Beach, to the marina. She always used to say sailing was like therapy." Killian pauses. "Of course, if Maxi had followed her down there . . . well, she might be alive today."

I can barely find my voice. "Oh my God," I whisper.

"Indeed. It's quite the burden for the old boy to bear."

I start to chew on my thumbnail but make myself stop and instead twist and knead my napkin in my lap. This explains so much about Max's dark moods, the incident at the cliff, everything. He's not just grieving her death—he feels responsible for it.

"You look like you could use a drink," Killian says gently.

"What? No. I'm fine."

"Let me get you something stronger than that Coke. They never card me here. They're marvelously European that way."

"No, honestly, I'm okay."

Killian gestures to the waiter, but I'm barely paying attention because my mind is racing a mile a minute. Why didn't Max tell me all this himself? Does he not trust me?

For that matter, why didn't Devon tell me? Or maybe she doesn't know.

"Here, drink this," Killian says, putting a glass in front of me.

Numb, I pick it up and take a sip. It tastes fizzy and fruity.

"I feel dreadful. I wanted to show you a good time today, and here I am, all doom and gloom," Killian says. "Listen, I'm having a few people over tonight. Eight o'clock. Why don't you come by? I promise it will cheer you up."

My brain feels weirdly spinny. "Thanks, but I can't."

"Just think about it, okay? Chapin Hall, room 333. Tell the guard that you're with me. He and I have an understanding. Oh, and Tess?"

I take another sip. "Hmm?"

"I'm sure you and Maxi have one of those wholesome relationships where you don't keep any secrets from each other. But a word of advice? I wouldn't mention this little lunch to him. Or my party, for that matter."

I perk up. More information. "Why not?" I ask, intrigued.

"I always thought of Maxi as a dear friend. But I don't think the feeling is mutual. He resented how close Becky and I were. I don't know if you know this about your boyfriend, but he's an extremely jealous person. Some would say pathologically so."

I gape at Killian. He shrugs and grins at me. *"Cherchez la femme,"* he says cheerfully. "Another round?"

28.

"I THOUGHT YOU WERE COMING TO THE GAME TODAY," MAX SAYS.

"What?"

"My soccer game. At two?"

How could I have forgotten? I am such an idiot.

Max and I are in Books and Beans, the library café. He texted a little while ago and asked if we could meet there. I was excited to hear from him but nervous, too, because of what Killian told me earlier.

Outside the window, the sky is oppressive, the color of an oil slick. It's only five o'clock, but the day feels like it's already over. The only other customer is a young guy wearing headphones, humming quietly to himself.

I fidget and take a sip of my bitter-tasting cappuccino. I

can't say anything about my lunch with Killian. Or that the drink Killian ordered for me made me really sleepy and spacey.

"I'm so, so sorry! I wasn't feeling well, and I lay down, and by the time I woke up, it was, like, hours later," I say instead.

Max looks concerned. "Are you better now?"

"I am. I really am sorry. I should have called you or texted you." I reach across the table and squeeze his hand. "Did you guys win?"

"Yeah. Score was close, 2–1."

"Congratulations!"

"Thanks. I wish I'd played better, though."

His phone beeps, and he glances at the screen. "Sorry, I've got to . . . It's Franklin, and I told him I'd . . ." He sighs wearily and starts texting.

I watch him as he types. He is so handsome. And sweet. And mysterious. I think of how Killian described him—mood swings, high maintenance, pathologically jealous. Yeah, the mood swings, definitely. But that's totally understandable, given the circumstances of Becca's death. And given that he's still grieving over her, as much as I hate to admit it.

But Killian said that Max was moody and high mainte-nance and all that *before* Becca died. Could that be true? And what about this jealousy business? I don't think I've ever seen that side of him.

And Killian said that Max resented Killian's relationship with Becca. Is that what Franklin was alluding to when he said I shouldn't discuss Killian with Max? Killian said the same thing to me at lunch.

Max slips his phone into his pocket. "Sorry 'bout that."

"How's Franklin?"

"He's, you know, Franklin."

I laugh. "What does that mean?"

"He's kind of overprotective. I didn't sleep great last night, and I was off my game today. So he's checking up on me. Which is nice of him, I guess, but totally unnecessary."

"Why didn't you sleep well?" I ask worriedly.

"Bad dreams. I guess I woke Franklin up."

"What kind of bad dreams?" I ask him hesitantly. I think about my own weird dream earlier this week, where I was alone on the beach and couldn't find him. I think about Becca. Was he dreaming about her?

"You know. Scary monster stuff," he jokes. "Seriously, it's no big deal."

I bite my lip in frustration. I wish that he would open up to me more.

Nearby, the guy with the headphones gets up to leave. He catches my eye. "Oh, hey!"

I have no idea who he is. "Um, hey?"

He slips off his headphones. "I saw you at that French restaurant today. I was having lunch with my girlfriend at the next table."

I feel the color draining from my cheeks. "Oh, right."

"Restaurant? What restaurant?" Max asks me curiously.

"Nice to see you again. Take it easy." The guy slips his headphones back on and exits the café.

"What restaurant?" Max repeats. His voice has an edge to it.

I plaster on a fake smile while I frantically improvise. "That French place you took me to. Devon kind of had this crisis . . ."

Max frowns.

"And she asked me to have lunch with her so I could give her advice and stuff," I finish lamely. "We would have met up at the cafeteria, but she said she needed to get away."

"So that's why you missed my game?"

"Yes. I'm really sorry."

"Why did you lie and say you weren't feeling well? You should have just told me the truth."

The truth. At this point, I'm fabricating on so many levels that I can barely keep my stories straight. "I know. I was afraid to because I thought you'd be mad. You don't exactly seem like a big fan of hers."

"Yeah, well . . ." Max turns away and gazes out the window.

"Max? Why is that?" I lean forward and reach for his hand.

I want so badly to feel close to him, but I don't want to scare him away, either. "Is it because she and Becca were best friends and you don't want to be reminded of her? Or—"

Max pulls his hand away, his dark eyes blazing. "Yeah, that's right. I don't want to be reminded of her. So let's drop the subject, okay?" He stands up abruptly and grabs his backpack. "I've gotta go."

"Max!"

"I'll call you tomorrow, okay?"

"Please, Max! What did I do?"

"Nothing. You didn't do anything." He takes off.

Watching him go, I struggle to fight back tears. Why do I keep blowing it with him?

And what's going to happen if he finds out I *didn't* have lunch with Devon?

29.

Back at Kerrith, I find Devon in our room. For once, I'm actually glad to see her.

"I need a huge favor," I say immediately.

She's lying on her bed in her underwear, flipping through *Vogue* and painting her nails dark purple. "Oh? What's the matter, did you and lover boy have a fight?" she asks, sounding bored.

"How did you know?"

Devon glances up. "I'm psychic. Did he finally get a clue and dump you for someone with more fashion sense?"

"No!"

I must sound semi-hysterical, because she suddenly looks concerned. "Hey, what's up? Are you okay?"

"I'm fine. Well, no, I'm not fine, but listen, I kind of lied to Max and told him we went out for lunch today."

Devon grins. "Wow, I'm proud of you! I didn't think you had it in you. So who *did* you have lunch with? Somebody super-hot, I hope."

"It's not important. Just . . . if Max says anything to you, will you back me up? Just tell him that you and I had lunch at that French place in town. At noon. You asked me to meet you there last minute because you were having a crisis."

"Awesome. What kind of crisis?"

"It doesn't matter. He and I didn't get into that."

Devon cocks her head. "So is that what you two had a fight about?"

I hesitate. I don't want to tell her any more than I have to. I barely trust her as it is. "Not exactly. It's complicated. But please . . . can you just do this thing for me?"

"Yes, but only if you do *me* a favor."

"What?"

"Killian Montgomery is having another party tonight. You can be my date. The girls have some lame art opening for their sculpture class. Besides, it's time you got out more."

Killian's party. There's no way I can go. Based on what Killian said, Max might lose it if he finds out.

"I can't."

"Why, do you and Max have plans?"

"No, but—"

"Then you'll come with me. Otherwise, your boyfriend is going to get an earful about how you begged me to cover your ass."

"Devon!"

She smiles her dazzling smile. "And that's how the game is played, Young Apprentice. Come on, let's get you out of that hideous outfit and into something more glamorous."

I clench my fists. "God, why are you such a *bitch*?" I burst out.

Devon's smile fades. "My, you *are* growing up!" she says coolly. "Good for you. Next thing you know, you'll be throwing punches at me."

"Whatever." I really can't deal with Devon's nastiness right now.

"Come on, I'm serious. Can we at least switch out the farm girl flannel for a decent top?"

"Yes, fine," I say wearily.

Someday, I'm just going to come right out and say no to Devon. Someday.

We knock on Killian's door at a few minutes after eight. My heart is racing and my palms are sweaty because I'm convinced that any second now, we'll run into Max and all hell will break loose.

But so far, so good. Devon and I made it into Chapin and up to the third floor without a single Max sighting or other mishap.

The door opens. Killian beams at us. "Ah! The two loveliest stars in the Thorn Abbey galaxy! Come in, come in."

"Hello, Killian." Devon kisses him on both cheeks.

"Hello, Devon. That dress is to die for. Hello, Tess!" Killian leans very close to me as I pass him in the doorway. "I'm delighted to see you," he whispers in my ear. He smells spicy. "Whatever made you change your mind?"

Blackmail, I want to say. "Oh, you know. I was in the mood for a party," I reply with a casualness I don't feel.

"Well, you've come to the right place. Let me give you the royal tour."

He hooks his arm through mine and leads me into his room. Or, I should say, palatial suite. It's twice as big as Devon's and my room. At least. Several dozen people are milling around, and I recognize some of them from around campus. They're all talking and laughing and drinking wine out of plastic cups while trumpety jazz throbs in the background. Louis Armstrong, maybe?

Devon has already sidled up to tall, hunky Jamal from my American history class. Killian presses a cup into my hand. "Here, my love. The presentation is a little lackluster. But it's a 1990, which was a fabulous year for the Alsatian whites."

I take a sip. It's cold and sweet. "So, um, Killian? I'm won-dering, sorry if this is awkward, but can you not mention to Devon that you and I had lunch?" I take a long drink.

"Of course! My lips are sealed." He glances over at Devon. "So are you two . . . ? I mean, I had presumed that you were quasi-exclusive with Maxi, but . . ."

"What? *No!* Devon is my *roommate,*" I sputter. Is he seriously suggesting that Devon and I are a couple?

"What an odd coincidence. She and Becky used to be roommates too. Devon didn't mention you to me."

"Oh."

"Forgive my nosiness, but why is it that we can't reveal our little rendezvous to her?"

"Oh, just because." I sigh and finish off the rest of my cup. Killian is right: This Alsatian whatever is pretty tasty. And it makes me feel tingly. "I wasn't going to tell Max about our lunch at all. But then we ran into the guy who was at the next table over, who said something about it to me, and then I had to lie to Max and tell him I was there with Devon. And then I had to ask Devon not to tell Max. And I didn't want to tell Devon I was with you because . . . well . . . I don't know. I don't trust her. Plus she scares me."

Killian laughs. "You are so refreshingly candid! It's a rare quality in this shark-infested sea of fakes and wannabes."

Candid. That's kind of hilarious, considering that I'm lying to pretty much everyone in my life right now. Including him. He thinks I came to his party of my own free will. "Thanks. But I'm beginning to think that I don't belong here. At Thorn Abbey, I mean."

"Of course you do! You just haven't met the right people. Even sharks can be amusing. Useful, too. Come, let me introduce you around. And let me freshen that for you."

Killian takes my cup and hands me another one. Whatever's in it tastes different, less Alsatian, more fiery. He walks me around the crowded room, air-kissing everyone, telling me about this person and that person: *His family practically owns Hollywood. . . . She's related to the Bahraini royal family. . . . Oh, and did I mention my famous New Year's Eve party at the Plaza last year?* I'm not taking in a lot of it, because my head is kind of fuzzy and reeling.

At one point, Killian introduces me to two girls named Mandy and Rae. Or Randy and Mae. One of them blows a smoke ring in my face, and the other giggles hysterically. Louis Armstrong isn't playing his trumpet anymore. A woman, Billie Holiday maybe, is singing about how her man doesn't love her.

Max, Max . . . where are you? I wonder forlornly.

And then suddenly—or it seems like suddenly, anyway—

Killian and Mandy/Randy are no longer there; it's Devon, and her hands are on my hips, and we're swaying to the music and dancing. "Having a good time?" she asks me.

"W-what?"

"I take that as a yes. You're definitely growing up. I'm impressed."

"Um, thanks?"

"But a word of caution?" Devon moves closer to me. "You will never replace her," she whispers fiercely. "Do you understand?"

"Replace who?"

She smiles at me coldly.

Then kisses me on the mouth.

Her lips—her bloodred lips—taste like cherries.

I have no idea what time it is as I stagger across the quad toward Kerrith. I'm probably in violation of curfew, or close to it, anyway. Everything is blurry: the buildings, the grass, the trees. *I'm drunk*, I tell myself. *I'm really, really drunk.*

Surely I will get busted—by Mrs. What's-Her-Name the house counselor and by the Kerrith security guard—and sent home to Avery Park. Which is just as well. Thorn Abbey is too, too confusing. It's like living in a fun house. Or a foreign country. Or a fun house in a foreign country. Or a fun house in a foreign country in an alternate universe.

I'm totally not making any sense.

My feet are freezing. I look down. I'm not wearing any shoes. Where on earth did I leave them? At that boy's party?

"Tess?"

Someone is calling my name. Maybe it's that boy, with my shoes. I spin around on my toes like a ballerina. But no one's there.

Although . . . there appears to be a person sitting on the steps of one of the buildings. Of Kerrith, actually. He gets up.

It's *him*. It's Max.

"Ohmigosh, hi," I say, waving. "What are you doing here?"

Max rushes up to me and hugs me, practically crushing me in his arms. "I've been texting you and calling you and looking for you everywhere," he murmurs. "I wanted to apologize."

"You . . . what? Why?"

He steps back and stares at me—and then at my feet. "Tess. Are you drunk?"

"Maybe a tiny bit." I forgot how cute he was.

"God. This is all my fault."

"No, it snot," I slur. "I mean, it's *not*."

"Yes, it is. I made you upset. When we met up for coffee at the library."

Library, library . . .

"Listen. I haven't been totally honest with you about stuff, because I was afraid," he confesses. "I still am."

Above us, I see a cloud passing across the moon.

"Maybe someday I can tell you everything. But right now, I need you to know that I care about you. I want to be with you, Tess. That is, if you still want to be with me."

"Oh!"

A small epiphany sparks to life in the dark, alcohol-soaked recesses of my brain: This is the moment I've been waiting for.

"I want to be with you, too," I say.

Max smiles and takes me in his arms again. He kisses me—deeply, hungrily. I can still taste Devon's cherry gloss on my lips.

I lean into his kiss. An owl hoots mournfully.

I'm in love.

PART TWO

30.

THE LAST TIME I CELEBRATED VALENTINE'S DAY WAS WHEN I was in second grade and the teacher made us pass out those store-bought cards to everyone in class—the ones that say BE MINE and HAVE A BEARY GOOD VALENTINE'S DAY! and stuff like that. Other than that, it was pretty much just my mom and me, watching romantic old movies on TCM and eating too many Russell Stover chocolates.

Which is why I can't wait for Valentine's Day this year. Thorn Abbey has an annual costume ball, and Max asked me to go with him.

"Mom, I need some sort of cool dress to wear to the ball," I tell her on the phone. "Cool but costumey. Something vintage or maybe even historical. Isn't there something in the attic, like in one of those old trunks?"

Across the room, Devon, studying-slash-eavesdropping on her bed, makes a gagging motion with her finger. I roll my eyes at her.

"Honey, those old trunks are full of magazines from the nineties and other crap I haven't gotten around to throwing away," my mom is saying. "I can poke around at the consignment shops for you, though. Oh, and the Salvation Army thrift store, too."

"Okay, thanks. I checked the stores in town, but I didn't find anything I liked. Besides, everything's super-expensive here."

"So are you going to this dance with your friends? Or with that boy you told me about at Christmas? How are things going with him?"

I hesitate. I don't want to say anything, especially with Devon sitting right there.

"Things are fine," I tell my mom quickly. "Listen, I have to run. Tons of homework! I'll e-mail you, okay? If you find any good dresses, can you text me pictures?"

"Will do. Love you!"

"Love you too, Mom." I hang up.

Devon glances up from her textbook. "Inverse functions suck," she mutters. "So you're dress hunting long-distance, huh?"

"I need something to wear to the costume ball."

"What about one of your usual outfits? You could go as a gender-confused hillbilly."

"Yeah, or I could borrow one of *your* usual outfits and go as a hooker," I banter back.

Devon grins. "Ha-ha. Hey, speaking of." She sets aside her textbook and reaches across the bed for her laptop. "*What* was the name of that website?" she mutters as she types. "I saw something the other day that might work for you. How do you feel about the slutty Victorian barmaid look?"

"That's not me."

"I know it's not you. That's the whole point of a costume ball. You told your mom that you wanted something historical."

"I'd prefer something more, you know, elegant."

"Well, Victorian barmaids can be elegant. In a slutty sort of way."

"You would know."

"Bitch!"

"Bitch!"

We crack up.

"*Ow!*" Devon stops laughing all of a sudden and rubs her temples.

"What's the matter?" I ask worriedly.

She closes her eyes and doesn't answer.

"Devon?"

"Hmm?" She opens her eyes and blinks slowly.

"Hey, are you all right?"

"This, uh, headache just hit me."

"I'm sorry. Do you want some Advil?"

"No, thanks." Devon turns to me with a tired smile. "Listen, I just thought of the perfect costume for you."

"You did? What is it?"

"Don't ask questions. Follow me." She stands up and holds her hand out to me. She looks a little pale.

I'm confused. But pleased. Devon wants to help me. "What about your headache? Are you sure you're up for—"

"Yes! Don't ask questions. Come on, before I change my mind."

"Okay."

I smile eagerly. This is going to be the best Valentine's Day ever.

It's been almost four months since Killian's party, when I kind of lost myself. From what I can remember, anyway. Since then, Max and I have been together and drama free. More or less.

After that party, I made a big decision. I decided to stop obsessing about Becca. I didn't like the jealous, crazy girl I'd turned into. I wanted to be the girl I used to be, before Thorn Abbey, but better. Braver. More confident.

I haven't looked inside Devon's silver box since I peeked in Becca's diary, ages ago. I've stopped cyber-stalking Becca—and Max and Killian, too. When Devon or the girls or anyone mentions Becca, I tune it out and think about other stuff.

It's better this way. My mom read this book once that said your thoughts become your reality. It's hokey, I guess, but I have to admit that it's sort of true. I don't let Becca occupy space in my brain, so her memory no longer has power over me.

I also told Killian that I couldn't hang out with him anymore. He tried to talk me out of it until I explained that I couldn't keep our friendship from Max any longer. When I said that, Killian's expression got all weird and inscrutable. He promised he would "be a gentleman" and keep his distance from me.

Not sure what that was about. But I'm glad Killian backed off so easily.

Another major change is Devon. She's been way less intense lately. I think it has to do with this guy she's been dating, Leo. Plus I came across some new medications on her dresser a while back, prescribed by a Dr. Caitlin Brennan. I looked them up online, and they're for sleep disorders, anxiety, and depression. They must be working, because she's definitely not as bitchy and bossy as she used to be. And she doesn't have her sleep-talking spells anymore either. Thank God.

There haven't been any scary noises, unexplained temperature changes, fireballs, glowing seagulls, or other "paranormal activity," as Kayleigh would say, not that I believe in ghosts. Still, I'm glad everything's as normal as it can be at Thorn Abbey.

With one exception. After the Christmas holiday, we all returned to find that someone had trashed the Kerrith third-floor lounge. One of the couches had been slashed. Shattered glass from the broken poster frames covered the floors. Graffiti defaced the walls. There was a single recognizable word in the chaos of spray paint:

OBEY

They haven't caught who did it yet. Devon was devastated, especially since the lounge renovation had been her idea. The entire third floor chipped in to help clean up.

After midterms in March, Devon, Yoonie, Elinor, Priscilla, and I are going shopping together for a replacement couch. I'm one of the girls now. Kind of a fifth wheel, but still. It's nice to know that I'm finally, truly starting to fit in.

⚜ ⚜ ⚜

Devon and I head down a long corridor in the east wing of Lanyon Hall. It's completely deserted except for a janitor swishing a mop across the wooden floor. He scowls at the clumps of snow we tracked in with our boots.

Dozens of large portraits, all in ornate gold frames, line the ruby-colored walls.

"I didn't even know this place existed," I whisper.

"I know, right? It's all offices back here, no classrooms. So normally, it's just Headmaster Henle and the other tedious grown-ups. And why are you whispering?"

"Sorry!" I raise my voice. "I feel like I'm in a museum or something. What's up with these paintings?"

"They're historical figures connected to Thorn Abbey. Or whatever. The point is, I remember one of them wearing this awesome dress. If you like it, we could try to find one that's similar."

"Oh! Great idea."

"I told you."

We continue down the corridor, checking out the portraits. There's Lucy Mosier, the first female student at Thorn Abbey, which apparently started as an all-boys school. There's Theodosia Dodd, the first headmistress. There are a bunch of well-known alumni—or is it alumnae?—that is, women who went to the school ages ago and then became famous.

"It's this one." Devon points to a portrait at the end of the corridor.

I glance at it. The woman in the portrait looks strangely familiar. She's beautiful, with golden hair cascading in soft waves to her waist.

"It's Aurora Thorn. She and her husband—" Devon starts to say.

"Augustus founded Thorn Abbey," I interrupt breathlessly. "That's where Max first kissed me! At the *Eternal Spirit* statue!'" I clamp my hand over my mouth. "I didn't mean to tell you. . . . I mean, it was kind of a private thing between Max and me, and . . ."

"Oh, for God's sake, Tess. Don't worry. Your boring G-rated secret is safe with me." Devon peers closely at the portrait. "So what do you think of the dress? It's pretty, right?"

The dress is pearly gray with a long, flowy skirt. It's incredibly romantic. "I've already decided. I'm definitely wearing this to the ball!"

"Are you sure? There's also that black dress over there—the one on the headmistress lady. It's kind of got a dominatrix vibe, doesn't it?"

"I'm one hundred percent sure."

I pull my phone out of my pocket and snap a couple of

pictures of Aurora Thorn's portrait. "Now I just have to find a dress like this somewhere."

"I can help you look. I need to find a dress for me, too. Maybe we can try online."

"Really? Thanks! I love you!" I give Devon an impulsive hug.

"Don't thank me yet. And you should definitely have a backup. You know, in case this style isn't flattering and you end up looking like a pregnant elephant."

Okay, so maybe the declaration of love was a bit premature.

31.

"WHY WON'T YOU TELL ME WHAT YOU'RE WEARING TONIGHT?"
Max asks me on the phone.

"Because it's supposed to be a surprise." I giggle.

I wedge my cell between my ear and my shoulder as I gaze
at myself in the mirror. I look exactly like Aurora Thorn—well,
maybe not *exactly* like her, but close enough.

Devon got me a dress that's basically identical to the one in
the painting. She found it at a vintage clothes store in Boston
last weekend when she was at home for a wedding. I had to
shorten it a little and use some safety pins here and there to give
me some breathing room, but otherwise, it's perfect. I borrowed
Priscilla's curling iron to make my hair wavy like Aurora's. I also
bought a white silk rose at a craft shop, cut off the plastic stem,

and fastened it to my hair with a bobby pin to look like the statue. For shoes, I splurged on some silver ballet flats at H&M.

"Well, I can tell you what I'm wearing," Max says. "A tux and cowboy boots."

"What are you supposed to be?"

"A guy in a tux and cowboy boots, obviously."

I laugh. "I'm sure you look really cute."

"I would prefer 'hot,' but yeah, okay."

We talk for a few more minutes before saying good-bye. We've agreed to meet at the dance, which is in Bolton Gym. I'm secretly planning to arrive a few minutes late. That way, I can make my grand entrance as "Aurora Thorn" with other people around. I can't wait for Max's reaction when he sees me. It's totally going to remind him of the first time we kissed. *So* romantic.

It's already seven fifteen p.m. I have about fifteen minutes to put on my makeup: mascara, blush, and peach lipstick. Devon already left about an hour ago, wearing her pink fairy princess costume, which is so not her, but which she somehow pulled off. She said something about hitting a preparty with Yoonie, Priscilla, and Elinor before meeting up with Leo at the dance.

I glance at Devon's bed, at the red heart-shaped pillow with the word "LOVE" embroidered in hot pink. It was an early Valentine's Day present from Leo. Devon hates it, though. She called it "cheesy" and complained bitterly because he didn't buy her jewelry instead.

I start to apply mascara, angling the bristly little brush the way Devon taught me to do. My eyes look a little tired. Devon's sleep-talking spells started up again a few days ago. One night, she was actually crying and saying "No, please don't make me!" over and over. I was so freaked out that I got up and tried to wake her. She hissed at me like an angry cat and immediately passed out. It was the weirdest thing.

I tried to talk to her about it the next day, but she said she didn't want to discuss it and changed the subject.

I wonder if she needs to switch her medications?

I blink into a white tissue to remove the excess mascara. I finish with the blush and lipstick and take one last look in the mirror. Perfect. I grab my parka, purse, and flats and waltz out the door.

As I leave, a faint, pleasant fragrance wafts around me. Is it coming from my dress? Devon said she had it dry-cleaned after she bought it. The scent is lovely and floral and somehow familiar. I hurry down the stairs, humming happily to myself.

Tonight will be unforgettable.

Bolton Gym is already crowded when I arrive. There are kings, queens, mermaids, superheroes, and an assortment of other characters. One boy is dressed as Mr. Bagley and is carrying around a copy of *The Norton Anthology of English Literature*. Several girls from Kerrith are dressed as Mrs. Frith. Shimmery red and pink heart decorations hang from the ceiling and on the walls. On the stage, a DJ is spinning "Slow Ride," which I recognize from Guitar Hero, and a bunch of students are gyrating under a silver disco ball. Headmaster Henle must have picked out the music again.

I stuff my parka into the jam-packed coatrack, pull off my boots, and slip into my flats. I look around for Max but don't see him anywhere. I don't see Devon or Leo or the girls, either.

"Tess? Is that you?"

I turn just as a musketeer greets me with a sweeping bow. The brim of his massive hat obscures his face.

Is it Franklin? It sounded like him. "Um, hi! Are you Athos, Porthos, Aramis, or D'Artagnan?" I ask cheerfully.

He removes his hat. It *is* Franklin, smiling at me.

Then he looks me up and down, and his smile disappears. "What in God's name do you think you're doing?" he demands.

Where did *that* come from?

"I'm waiting for Max. And making pretentious Alexandre Dumas references. What are *you* doing?"

"You have to go change. *Now*," he hisses.

"What? Why?" I glance down worriedly. "I haven't spilled anything on my dress," I add.

215

That's when I spot Max coming up from behind Franklin. He looks stunning in his suave black tuxedo and silly cowboy boots.

His face lights up when he sees me . . .

. . . then turns deathly pale. He stares at my dress with unmasked horror.

What is happening?

I grab his arm. "Max, what's wrong?"

His jaw clenches and unclenches. He doesn't say a word.

"I'm *her*!" I remind him with a desperate smile. "Aurora Thorn! Remember the *Eternal Spirit* statue? Where we first kissed?"

Max dips his head toward my neck. At first I think he's going to whisper something in my ear. But he breathes deeply, and I realize he's smelling me.

"Her dress *and* her perfume? Tess, how could you?" he cries out furiously. "I have no idea what kind of sick joke this is, but—I'm out of here. We're through. Do you understand me?"

"*Max!*" I shout.

He takes off. I start to run after him, but Franklin catches my hand. "Tess, let him go."

I burst into tears. "Franklin, what did I *do*?" I wail.

"Are you serious? This is the exact same dress that Becca wore to the ball last year. With Max."

I'm so stunned, I can't find my voice.

"Of all the costumes you could have picked, why this one?" Franklin says angrily. "Didn't you know how it would make him feel? How did you even know what Becca wore last year?"

"But I didn't—"

Devon. It was all Devon's idea. She totally set me up.

But why? The whole thing is insane.

I head toward the exit. "Where are you going?" Franklin calls after me.

"Just leave me alone!" I yell.

People are staring at me.

I don't care.

Max and I are so over.

My life is so over.

32.

Whitwater Beach. I haven't been here since September, when I found Max standing on the edge of the cliff.

I don't know why I came back here. It's like some mysterious force propelled me across the snowy quad, through the woods, and back to this awful, desolate place. Maybe a part of me thought I would find some peace. Or maybe I thought I would find Max.

But no. There's nothing here but the full moon and icy wind. And the ominous sight of waves crashing and pounding against the rocks a hundred feet below.

I stand on the cliff, gazing numbly down at the beach. I'm usually afraid of heights, but I don't feel any fear right now—just despair. In the distance, to the south, I can just make out the marina and the trail leading down to it.

I imagine Becca and Max taking long walks on the beach, their heads bent together. Or them lying on a blanket, kissing and caressing.

I imagine the two of them on their date last May. I imagine them arguing, her running off. I imagine her hurrying down to the marina and taking out one of the boats. I imagine the wind picking up and snapping the sails. I imagine her terror as the storm intensified and swells battered the hull. I imagine her boat capsizing. I imagine her drowning.

She died that night, and yet, she's not dead. Because no matter how hard I try to fight her, she's in my head. Under my skin. And tonight, I'm even wearing her dress and her perfume.

I step closer to the edge.

Footsteps crunch in the snow behind me.

"Max?" I turn, feeling sick with hope.

But it's not Max. It's Devon, a glamorous fur coat draped carelessly over her pink fairy princess gown. She's carrying my parka and a bottle of something.

"Get back from there, you idiot!" she orders me.

"Go away! I *hate* you!" I scream. I must look crazy: standing in the freezing cold in Becca's dress, mascara streaking down my face. But I don't care.

"Tess, don't be stupid. Let me explain."

"This is *all* your fault! You made me wear Becca's dress so

Max would freak out and break up with me. *Why?* Why would you do this to me? Why now?"

"Tess!" Devon drags me back from the precipice. She thrusts my parka at me. "For God's sake, put this on. You're going to catch pneumonia."

"I don't care!"

"Max is still in love with her."

I flinch. "What are you talking about?"

"I tried to tell you before, ages ago. But you wouldn't listen."

"You're wrong!" I close my eyes and try to understand what Devon is saying. It makes no sense. "Besides, what does that have to do with tonight?"

"He came to see me a few weeks ago. He was drunk. He wanted to talk to me about Becca."

No.

"He said he couldn't stop thinking about her. He said he thought he could move on, with you. But he can't. He was beside himself."

No, no, no. Max wouldn't betray me like this.

"I knew you wouldn't believe me if I told you," Devon continues. "I had to show you how he felt. You were so focused on finding the perfect dress for the dance, and Becca had this replica made in Philadelphia, just for last year's ball. I still had it in my closet, from after she died. So I convinced you to wear it. I didn't realize you and Max had your first kiss at the statue and all that."

"That's insane," I whisper.

"I don't blame you for being pissed off. But I had to make you see. If Max didn't care about Becca anymore, he wouldn't have remembered the damned dress."

I glare at her. "How do you even know what happened at the dance? You weren't there."

"Franklin told me everything, so I went to find you. I saw you from a distance, and then I tracked your prints in the snow from the trail. Aren't I clever?"

"No, you're *not* clever. You're horrible."

"I didn't want to keep seeing you get hurt. You might not think so, but you're my friend."

I feel my body trembling. I'm crying again. Or maybe I'm freezing to death. Whatever.

"Oh, sweetie." Devon wraps my parka around my shoulders and hands me the bottle. "Here, drink this. It will warm you up."

"What is it?" I ask suspiciously.

"Trust me, you need it."

I take a tentative sip. Whatever it is tastes like honey and fire and burns all the way down my throat. I take another, longer drink.

"I thought he loved me," I moan.

"That asshole! He told you he *loved* you?"

"No, he never *told* me using those words. I figured he was just waiting for the right moment."

"Oh, sweetie," Devon repeats with a heavy sigh.

"I've never been in love before, do you know that? I've never even had a real boyfriend. And then I met Max. At first I thought there was no way I could ever compete with Becca because I wasn't pretty enough or clever enough or popular enough. But Max told me he liked me for me. He *said* so. Was he lying?"

Devon takes a sip from the bottle too. "It's a guy thing. They say stuff like that."

"But Max isn't just any guy."

"In some ways, no. But in other ways, he's just like the rest of them."

"I don't believe it!"

"Believe it. It sucks, being in love with someone who doesn't love you back. I've been there." Devon smiles bitterly. "Drink up."

We stand near the cliff for a while, trading the bottle back and forth, listening to the roar of the sea. Does love always hurt like this? Like your insides have been ripped out, like you've been staked through the heart? If so, I never want to fall in love again. Ever. I'd rather spend the rest of my life alone.

I'm not sure how much time passes. Minutes? Hours? The bottle of honey-fire is almost empty. Devon starts telling me a story about a girl she once knew. A girl *she* used to love . . .

But I'm not paying attention because someone else is talking to me now: *Max doesn't want you. Nobody wants you. Why don't you just disappear?*

My head is spinning and whirling. I hear Devon calling my name.

"Tess!"

My legs give way.

"Tess! Grab my hand!"

I'm falling, falling into the abyss.

Someone laughs: a shrill, vindictive laugh.

Now *I'm* the one who's drowning.

33.

I AM WALKING DOWN THE PATH, THE ONE THAT WINDS THROUGH the woods by Thorn Abbey and leads down to the beach. The air is cool and wet with rain, and my footsteps are light on the carpet of brown fallen leaves as I hurry down to the place where I know he is waiting for me. My cheeks are cold, and my heavy wool sweater scratches against my skin, but I don't care, because I can already feel his strong arms around my body and his warm lips against mine.

And then I am at the bottom of the hill. The beach rises above the horizon, endless and gray. Suddenly I feel exposed. Frightened. The air is different here: bigger, less forgiving. It smells like the sea and salt and dead things.

I move closer to the water. A wave rushes up to my boots

and then snakes away, leaving two identical dark stains. I shudder against the chill and look around. Where is he, and why is he late?

Another wave comes up, more imposing than the last, and I step back. But the wave doesn't retreat. It keeps rising toward me, not cresting or breaking. I cry out and stumble backward. The wave grows larger, more menacing, finally overtaking me and sucking me into its icy deep.

Hands, fingers, hair. *Her* hands, her fingers, her hair. They wrap around me, colder than death, and pull me under as I scream. Her face—her beautiful, perfect face that he loved with a passion he will never feel for me—is the last thing I see as my lungs fill with the brackish water and I black out into the nothingness, still calling out his name in vain.

"*No!*" I shout, startling awake.

I'm shaking all over. My skin is hot and cold at the same time, and my head feels like a thick slab of cement.

Where am I? In bed. My bed. My sheets are sweaty and stale and tangled.

I have wispy memories of recent events. Or were they just dreams? The cliff. Devon half carrying me to the clinic. Coming back to Kerrith. Somebody feeding me broth, juice, saltines. Devon sitting beside me, stroking my hair with this creepy focus, like she was in a trance.

Then she was talking to someone, crying, pleading. But I don't remember anyone else being in the room.

I reach over to my nightstand and paw through the museum of my illness: wadded-up tissues, plastic cups, bottles of medicine, a thermometer.

Ah, there it is. My phone. The screen says it's 9:05 a.m. on February 17.

How surreal. Three days have somehow passed since that awful night. Three days of lying in bed, burning with fever, having the same terrible dream over and over again. The one where she's trying to kill me.

Unless it's not a dream?

Obviously, on top of everything else, the fever has gone to my brain and made me crazy, crazy, crazy.

I have a bunch of text messages. I scroll through the list groggily. There's a message from Devon telling me she's in class all day but that she'll check in on me around five. There are multiple get-well messages from Priscilla, Elinor, Yoonie, Franklin, even Killian, whom I haven't spoken to in ages. There are two voice mail messages from my mom, asking me if I'm feeling better and should she FedEx me some homemade chicken soup—or come to Thorn Abbey to take care of me?

There's nothing from Max, though. Not that I was expecting to hear from him ever again.

I slump back against my pillows, cradling my phone to my chest. *Now* what? Maybe I could transfer back to Avery Park High. It's mid-semester, but my mom could talk to Headmaster Henle and Principal Fowler at Avery Park and convince them. She could tell them there's a family emergency.

Or maybe I could just drop Mr. Bagley's seminar. That way, I wouldn't have to see Max anymore. Or much, anyway.

I'm so tired. I want to go back to sleep, except I'm terrified of dreaming that dream again. . . .

Max is standing over me.

"Tess? It's me," he says softly.

My eyelids flutter. "This is a much better dream," I mumble.

He cracks a smile. "You're not asleep. I'm here. In your room."

Oh. My. God. Max is in my room.

I sit up hastily and run a hand through my greasy, disgusting hair, which I haven't washed since Valentine's Day. "What are you doing here?" I ask in wonder.

"I was worried about you."

"Y-you were?"

"You weren't in Bags's class this morning. I asked Mrs. Frith, and she told me how sick you've been," Max explains.

"You asked her about me?"

"Yeah. She even gave me special permission to come up

for a few minutes, as long as I leave the door open. Listen, Tess . . ." Max sits down on the edge of my bed. He glances around; I can tell by his expression that he's rattled. It's probably been a while since he was in Becca's old room. The last time he was here, he and she were probably . . .

No, no. Don't think about that.

"Franklin told me. That you didn't know about the dress," Max says after a moment.

"He did?"

"I'm sorry I jumped to conclusions. It's just that, well . . . it's kind of a bizarre coincidence that you'd wear the exact same dress, right? What was I supposed to think?"

"But it *wasn't* a coincidence," I say quickly. "Devon still had the dress in her closet. I had no idea it was Becca's dress. She tricked me into wearing it. Because of what you told her."

Max frowns. "Because of what I told who?"

"Because of what you told Devon. A few weeks ago. About how you're still"—I drop my gaze, struggling to keep my voice level—"how you're still in love with Becca. Devon told me everything, after you left. She said she thought it would be a good reality check for me to wear the dress to the ball and see your, you know, *reaction.*"

"Are you fucking joking?"

I cringe. Why is Max so angry? Because Devon betrayed his

confidence? "No, of course I'm not joking! Devon told me how you came to her all drunk and depressed and missing Becca."

Max jumps to his feet and begins pacing around the room. His fists are knotted so tightly that his knuckles turn pure white.

"Max? What is it?" I ask him worriedly.

He whirls around. "Devon is a damned liar. I never had this conversation with her—not a few weeks ago, not ever."

"What?" I'm so confused. Who am I supposed to believe?

"And, more important, I'm not still in love with Becca because I've never *been* in love with Becca. She was the worst thing that ever happened to me," he spits out.

I stare at him, stunned. And ecstatic. Max doesn't love Becca. He never loved Becca.

Unless he's lying to me.

No, he looks totally sincere.

It takes me a long time before I can find my voice again. "I—I don't understand," I finally manage. "Devon said . . . I thought you and Becca were *the* couple on campus or whatever. Becca was beautiful and perfect, and you were obsessed with her."

"Yeah, she was beautiful," Max says. "And she *seemed* perfect, on the outside. If you met her, you'd think she was the sweetest, kindest, most together girl. Everyone loved her."

Ouch. "Why was she the worst thing that happened to you, then?"

"Because it was all an act. She was super-insecure, deep down. She craved constant attention. At parties, she would flirt with every guy in the room. Then we'd have a big fight about it afterward, and she would cry and apologize and tell me how she wanted me and only me."

I chew on my thumbnail. I'm relieved that Becca wasn't perfect, but this isn't exactly fun to hear.

"Our relationship only lasted for a few months. We started dating in January, February. I thought about breaking up with her. Several times, in fact. But every time I tried to talk to her, tell her things weren't working out, she'd cry and beg me to stay. She said she would change. And I believed her."

"Then what happened?"

"Then the accident happened." Max looks away and falls silent.

"Max?" I reach over and squeeze his hand. Killian told me how Becca died and how Max felt responsible for her death. The memory must still be so traumatic for him.

"We had another fight that night," Max continues, gazing out the window. "She took off for the beach, and that was the last time I saw her. There was a big storm that night, and she never came back to her room. One of the teachers found the boat onshore the next morning. Becca loved to sail, and she must have gone out by herself. The police found her body some time after that."

"I'm so sorry, Max," I say, meaning it.

"Yeah. Me too."

He doesn't speak for a long time. When he finally meets my eyes, he seems afraid. Haunted. I've never seen him like that before.

I wish I could ask him exactly what he is feeling. But he seems really upset now, and I don't want to push him.

I also have a million other questions. Like, why does Max still have that book of love poems Becca gave him? And why did Devon lie to me about Max's relationship with Becca?

Of course, Devon is the only one who can answer *that* question. As soon as I see her, I'm seriously going to strangle her with my bare hands.

"Listen, I'm sorry to dump all this on you," Max says quietly.

"No. I'm so glad you told me. I always thought Becca was this perfect girlfriend I could never live up to."

"Hardly." Max hesitates. "You know, I'm not perfect either. Far from it."

I smile. "You're perfect to me."

He smiles back—sadly, wearily. "I hope you'll always think so."

He cradles my face and kisses me. We sink back against the pillows, his hands caressing my white cotton nightgown. I barely even think about whether or not he used to kiss Becca like this, here, in this bed.

He's mine. He was never hers. He's mine, forever.

34.

I DON'T SEE DEVON FOR THE REST OF THE DAY. AROUND SIX, I consider texting her about why she didn't check up on me as promised, but I'm too mad to deal with her. Tomorrow. I'll be able to talk to her without killing her tomorrow.

I eat a box of saltines for dinner and turn in early. I'm actually feeling better. It must have been Max's visit. In the morning I might try walking over to the Lanyon Commons for real food.

Just before I fall asleep, Max sends me a text:

Can we celebrate Valentine's Day again? Dinner soon? Maybe Saturday if you're feeling up to it?

I smile and type:

Yes!!!!

I hug my phone to my chest as I switch off the light. In a funny way, this belated Valentine's Day dinner will be my first real date with Max. Because now I know the truth about him and Becca. I'll be able to sit across from him without wondering if he's lost in old memories, if he'd rather be with her than with me.

A brand-new beginning. I can't wait.

When I wake up the next morning, I see that Devon's bed hasn't been slept in. Where is she? Maybe she knows I'm furious with her and wants to avoid me.

For the first time in days, I feel strong enough to take a shower and get dressed. I grab my towel and tote, and I head down the hall to the bathroom.

Yoonie is at one of the sinks, brushing her teeth.

She spits. "Hey, you're alive. How *are* you? We were all super-worried."

"I feel like I had the black plague, though I'm way better, thanks. Listen, did Devon crash with you guys last night?"

"Noooo. I haven't seen her since, like, lunch yesterday," Yoonie replies.

Where could she be? "She didn't sleep in our room last night," I explain.

Yoonie puckers her lips and slides on red lip gloss. "She

probably slept over at Leo's. I think his roommate's out of town, and"—she smiles into the mirror—"you know our Devon. Do you want me to text her?"

"Sure, thanks."

Yoonie pulls her phone out of her pocket and types with one hand while poking at her eyelashes with the other. *Wow, that's talent.* I step into a shower stall and turn on the faucet. Soon I'm in a veritable paradise of hot water, Ivory soap, and strawberry shampoo. I haven't been this clean in nearly a week.

"Hey, Tess?" Yoonie calls out.

"Hmm?"

"She didn't text back, so I called her. It went straight to voice mail. Then I texted Leo. He says he hasn't heard from her either. Devon was supposed to meet up with him last night, and she never showed."

"What?" I rub the water out of my eyes and peer out from behind the shower curtain. "Where is she?"

"I don't know," Yoonie says worriedly. "But we should probably tell Mrs. Frith."

"Definitely."

Alarm bells are going off in my head. Why would Devon pull a disappearing act? Is she trying to get attention?

Or did something happen to her?

⚜ ⚜ ⚜

By the middle of the afternoon, both campus security and the local police are searching for Devon. Her parents haven't heard from her. No one's heard from her. The last time anyone saw her was just after lunch yesterday, when she told Señora Velásquez that she had to skip Spanish because she wasn't feeling well.

Mr. Correa from campus security and a police officer named Phibbs interviewed me about Devon, asking me all sorts of questions. I told them I had no idea where she could be. They asked me if any of her luggage or clothes or important documents, like her passport, were missing. I searched through her closet and dresser and desk—even under her bed. Everything was in order.

Except.

The medications in her dresser drawer—the ones she's been taking for sleep disorders, anxiety, and depression.

After Mr. Correa and Officer Phibbs left, I counted the pills in each bottle and checked the quantities against the dates on the labels.

Devon hasn't been taking her meds for at least a month, even though she's been taking her birth control.

I went online and it said that once you go off these drugs, they can stay in your system for several weeks, but then they start wearing off.

Devon's been pretty normal for the last four months, until the incident with Becca's dress.

Did she get weird again because she stopped taking her meds? Is she losing it?

I am walking down the path, the one that winds through the woods by Thorn Abbey and leads down to the beach. Yoonie, Elinor, and Priscilla are right behind me. It's nearly five, so we're all carrying flashlights and, of course, our phones.

We're one of the search parties combing the campus for Devon. Max and Franklin are part of another, crisscrossing the woods behind Lanyon Hall. There are a bunch of other students out searching too, as well as teachers, staff, and others.

"That bitch. She probably went down to New York City to shop and didn't tell us," Elinor says.

"Yeah. Or she checked into a hotel with Leo's hot roommate. He's not around either," Yoonie jokes.

"Y'all, this is serious. She's *missing*," Priscilla points out.

"Yeah, we know it's serious, Pris. I had to take an extra Klonie just to get through the day. *And* make an emergency call to my therapist," Elinor snipes.

It's so ironic. If it were any other occasion, I would be so happy being on an outing with the girls, listening to their chatter.

Granted, it's only been, like, twenty-four hours. And there

could be some truth to what Elinor and Yoonie said. If we're lucky, Devon is safe and sound somewhere, partying it up or spending lots of money. Or both.

I glance at the dusky sky through the canopy of bare branches. The sun is starting to sink to the horizon. It's been freakishly warm these last couple of days—high forties, low fifties. But it will be dark soon, and temperatures will drop. Luckily, Yoonie thought to pack a blanket and a thermos of hot coffee.

"We're almost at the beach," I say to the others. "If we don't find her there, there's another trail back to campus, right? By the marina? We can double back along that one and look for her."

"Oh, yeah. I think Killian and some of his lax bros are already covering it," Yoonie volunteers.

Elinor frowns at her loafers. "*Why* didn't somebody tell me to wear boots? I'm ruining my new Ferragamos."

"What, did you think we were going to a polo match?" Priscilla says, rolling her eyes.

I hurry my steps, barely registering the nonstop nervous bickering behind me. We pass the DANGER: NO HIKING BEYOND THIS POINT sign, and soon we are at the cliff.

I cross my arms over my chest and shudder. Was I really here less than a week ago? Sobbing my heart out in Becca's dress, thinking I'd lost Max forever? So much has changed between us. And between me and Devon. So much for her rescuing me with a bottle of liquor and her sage, sisterly advice. Pretending to be my friend.

I stare out at the breaking waves—and scream.

There is her body way below, sprawled on a thin stretch of beach. Or *a* body, anyway. Two arms, two legs, dark clothing.

"Devon?" I shout.

The body doesn't move.

Yoonie peers down. "Is that her? I can't tell from here."

"Is she dead?" Priscilla cries out.

"Don't even *say* that," Elinor whines.

I glance around frantically. "Does anyone know the fastest way down there?"

"Yeah. Jumping. Second fastest is this way. Follow me," Yoonie says.

She starts crab-walking along a narrow, rocky path that winds down the face of the cliff. "Be careful, it's slippery!"

We all follow. Behind me, I hear Priscilla calling 911. My brain is on total overload. I can't believe this is happening. This morning, I was ready to strangle Devon—not literally, but the sentiment was there. And now she may be lying dead on Whitwater Beach.

"I think it's just a piece of driftwood," Elinor says anxiously.

"Don't be clueless! That's a fucking *person*!" Yoonie yells over her shoulder.

We get to the bottom of the cliff. It *is* Devon. Lying face-down in the sand. I recognize her fur-trimmed black parka, which she once told me cost more than my entire wardrobe times ten.

"Devon!" I drop to my knees and flip her over carefully.

Her emerald eyes are wide open, like a dead fish. Her lips are blue.

I bend down to check if she's breathing.

She isn't.

Oh God, oh God, oh God . . .

"Oh, fuck! Get out of the way!" Someone pushes me aside roughly.

I tumble into a cold tide pool. Killian straddles Devon's body and rips open her parka. Behind him are three boys I don't recognize, all in long, baggy shorts, polos, and hoodies. They must have reached the base of their trail the same time we reached the end of ours.

Killian begins CPR. He alternates the pumping motions with mouth-to-mouth. "Come on, darling. Wake up!" he grunts at Devon as he presses down on her chest. "Did someone call 911?"

"Done. I'm gonna call campus security too," Yoonie says, reaching for her phone.

I watch, mesmerized. Killian the dilettante party boy is performing CPR like a trained medic.

"Dude, where'd you learn how to do that?" one of the other guys comments.

"Internship. Mass. General. Hospital," Killian pants. "Breathe, damn it!"

Elinor and Priscilla are clutching each other and crying. Yoonie is on the phone with security.

What happened to Devon? I can't help but think about Becca. She drowned in these waters too. It couldn't be a coincidence. Did Devon try to follow her best friend to the other side?

Devon's head jerks up suddenly. She vomits a spray of water, then gasps. Killian stops CPR and sits up, breathing hard.

"Devon! *Sweetie!*" Priscilla shrieks.

"Ohmigod, she's alive!" Elinor hugs one of the lacrosse players.

I rise slowly to my feet. But she was *dead*. She was definitely dead.

Devon blinks up at Killian. He gazes into her emerald eyes for what seems like forever.

"You're back," he says finally.

Devon smiles. "Hey, Monty," she whispers hoarsely. "Did you miss me?"

The deafening sounds of an EMS helicopter slice the air above us.

35.

DEVON SPENDS TWO NIGHTS IN THE HOSPITAL BEFORE
returning to Thorn Abbey. When she walks into our room, she
drops her bag, hugs me, and doesn't let go for a long time.

"You saved my life," she murmurs. "I owe you so much."

"Honestly, it was all Killian. Are you okay?" I step back and
study her face. She looks pale, tired, disoriented.

"I'm fine. Really. Everyone at the hospital was so nice
to me."

"Devon, I do wish you'd just come back to Boston with
me," a voice calls out from the doorway. "Dr. Schynoll says he'd
be happy to clear his schedule for you."

I glance past Devon. A tall woman in a stylish red coat is
standing in the doorway, scrolling briskly through her phone.

She looks just like Devon, except for her super-short haircut and chunky black glasses.

"But I really miss school! Please, Mother, can't I stay?" Devon pouts.

Devon's mom. "Hi, I'm Tess," I say, waving.

"I'm sorry! Tess, this is my mom, Cait McCain. Mother, this is my roommate, Tess," Devon says.

"It's Brennan now, remember? Dr. Brennan." She turns to me. "Hello, Tess."

Dr. Caitlin Brennan. That's the name on Devon's prescription bottles.

"Are you *sure* you're all right?" Dr. Brennan asks Devon with a frown.

"I'm fine! But you're super-sweet to worry," Devon replies.

"I don't think you've called me 'sweet' since you were four years old," Dr. Brennan remarks. "Okay, I'll be heading back, then. I have a huge backlog of patients. Will you please keep me posted on your progress? And remember to take your medications?"

"I will, Mother. Thanks so much for being here. I know how busy you are." Devon gives her a big hug.

"You're . . . welcome." Dr. Brennan pats Devon on the back as if she's surprised by Devon's affection. "I'm off. I'll text you when I get home."

"No, call me!"

"Yes, of course. I'll call you."

When the door closes, I turn to Devon. "Can I get you any-thing? Like a snack from the vending machine? A soda? Some real food?"

"No, I'm great. I'm just so happy to be back."

She walks around the room—slowly, almost timidly. She picks up a bottle of French rosewater from her dresser, sniffs it, and rubs a little on her wrists. She examines the posters on her wall. She sits down on her bed and runs her hand across the purple silk comforter.

At the hospital, Devon told the doctors, the police, every-one, that she cut classes on Monday after lunch because she had a headache and some "boy problems" to mull over. She decided to take a walk on the beach because it was so nice out.

She said she remembered going to the cliff. She remem-bered walking down the same narrow, rocky path that Yoonie, Elinor, Priscilla, and I went down, even though it was techni-cally off-limits. She remembered losing her footing and pan-icking. And then, nothing . . . until she woke up and saw Killian and the rest of us hovering over her before the helicopter whisked her away to the hospital.

The police ruled what happened an accident. Their theory is that Devon was close to the end of the path when she fell, tumbling down to the beach and losing consciousness. The doctors said it was a miracle that she didn't get washed out to sea at high tide or freeze to death. As it was, she only suffered a mild concussion, cuts, and bruises.

Devon picks up her stuffed red heart. "My pillow!" she says, kissing it.

Her pillow? She told me that she hated it. Why is she acting so bubbly? Did she switch personalities with a cheerleader?

"Are you sure you're okay?" I ask. I sound like her mother.

"I'm great! So what did I miss while I was gone?"

I shrug. "Not much."

"How are things with Max? Did you two have a nice Valentine's Day?"

"Excuse me?"

"You know. Valentine's Day. Did you do anything fun or romantic?"

What the hell?

"I'm sorry, you—you don't remember?" I stammer.

"Remember what?"

Devon smiles at me, waiting for my answer. I don't understand what's happening. Did the accident mess with her memory? She wasn't breathing when we found her. Was her brain deprived of oxygen for too long? Is she suffering from that post-traumatic stress thing people get? That might explain why she's acting like a totally different person.

"Um, yeah. We had a really nice Valentine's Day. Thanks for asking," I reply after a moment.

"You're welcome!" Devon clutches her LOVE pillow to her chest and rocks from side to side. "It is *so* awesome to be back. I hated being trapped."

"Trapped?"

"You know, in a hospital bed." She glances over at the pink laptop on my desk. "Is that mine?" she asks, confused.

"That's the computer you lent me. Becca's old computer, remember? Yours is probably in your backpack."

Devon's eyes widen. "Oh, right! I totally want to catch up on my e-mails and stuff. I probably have, like, a thousand of them."

She rises to her feet, goes to her desk, and starts digging through her backpack, humming a Taylor Swift song. But Devon *hates* country music. She bitched out Priscilla during lunch once for having Jason Aldean on her iPod.

I sit down at my desk and make myself busy as well. Or pretend to, anyway. My mind is racing. Why is Devon acting so bizarrely? I wonder if I should call the hospital, or her scary mom, or tell Mrs. Frith, or what?

36.

ON SATURDAY MORNING, MAX AND I HEAD OVER TO THE library to study for midterms. It had snowed overnight, and the entire campus is blanketed in pure, white stillness. Sunlight catches the ice crystals on tree branches and makes them glitter. It's all very magical and winter-wonderland, especially since Max and I are holding hands.

Except that he's not in the greatest mood.

"So how's the roommate from hell?" Max asks me. "Have you called her out about Valentine's Day yet? What lame excuses did she come up with?"

I kick at a snowdrift with my boots. "Actually, I haven't had a chance to talk to her," I admit. "I was waiting for her to get better. But she's been acting really weird."

"Yeah, so what else is new?"

"No, something's different. She broke up with Leo, for one thing. Like, totally out of the blue. And she's being super-nice to me and acting cheerful all the time," I explain.

Max shrugs. "She breaks up with guys all the time. Everyone knows she's hooked up with half the school. And she's probably being nice to you because she feels guilty about trying to break *us* up."

He sounds more annoyed than concerned. Not that I can blame him. I know he's still furious at Devon for what she did to us.

"She's also having memory lapses," I add.

"Memory lapses are normal, aren't they? After an accident like that?"

"I guess. I ran into Killian Montgomery the other day and mentioned it to him. He said it *is* pretty normal but that he'd talk to Devon's mom about it. I guess he knows her. She's a doctor."

Max's hand tightens around mine. "Killian Montgomery? So you're friends with him now?"

"No, not at all. He was just the one who performed CPR on Devon when we found her, and I know he's good friends with Devon, and . . ."

Ugh. It's been so long since I've had to lie to Max that I totally forgot *not* to mention Killian to him. Max and I have never actually discussed Killian. Much less the fact that he's Becca's cousin, even though everyone knows, obviously.

"Anyway, Devon seems fine otherwise," I babble on, hoping to distract him from asking about my conversation with Killian. "I think she might be on a lot of medications or something."

"I don't think meds will help. That girl is psycho," Max says fiercely.

"I'm sorry. Let's not talk about her anymore, okay?" I nestle against his arm. "Are we still on for our Valentine's Day dinner tonight?"

He kisses the top of my head. "If you're still up for it."

I've been looking forward to our dinner all week. It will be so nice to be with Max and just relax, particularly after all the crazy Devon drama.

"Yes! It'll be our own little private celebration. We're nine days late, but . . . who's counting?" I add, nudging him, playfully.

"Eight. Wow, you suck at math. How did you get into this school, anyway?" he jokes back.

"Ha-ha."

As we pass the stone fountain, I think about how my conversation with Max on Monday reset the clock for us. It's like we're starting from scratch with no bad karma, no obstacles. It's just the two of us now. From here on, there won't be a third person haunting our thoughts.

It doesn't even bother me anymore that the fountain is a tribute to Becca's memory. It's just an object. An inanimate thing. It can't hurt me.

Max stops and scoops his hand in the snow to make a snowball. He pitches it at the tall pillar. And misses.

"Wow, you suck at throwing," I say, pleased that the fountain seems to have lost its power over him, too.

He laughs and takes me in his arms. "That's because you're distracting me," he says, and kisses me passionately.

I am so, so happy.

The owner of the Danube Café hands me a laminated menu with a picture of the red, white, and green Hungarian flag at the top. With her silver-gray curls and white apron, she looks like someone's grandma.

"Tonight we have a beautiful Székely goulash special," she informs me in a thickly accented voice. "It has pork, paprika, sour cream, sauerkraut. Very delicious."

"Um, thank you."

She glances at the empty chair across from me. "Are you waiting for a friend?"

"Yes. My boyfriend."

She winks at me. "I will bring the two of you a special dessert later. A romantic dessert. Very delicious."

"That's really nice of you, thanks."

She leaves me to study the menu and wanders off to wait on other customers. I'm definitely a lot more comfortable in restaurants than when Max and I were first dating. By this time next year, maybe I'll be ready for dinner with the De Villierses again.

I lean back in my chair and scan the room. The Danube Café is cute and cozy, with brick walls and Hungarian folk art and travel posters of Budapest. It's also packed: There isn't a single empty table. I recognize a big group of Thorn Abbey students in the corner.

Max thought I would like this place since I'm part Hungarian, which is so thoughtful of him. Except . . . where *is* he? He texted me earlier and asked if he could meet me here instead of Kerrith. He said that something had come up.

I pick up my phone. He's almost fifteen minutes late. I take a sip of my Coke and type:

Where are you? I'm at the restaurant.

No reply. I wait another five minutes. Still no reply.

I decide to try Franklin next. He texts right back and says he thought Max was with me.

Nope.

Franklin texts again and says he's in for the night studying, and he'll let me know if Max shows up.

I gnaw on my thumbnail and dial Max's number. It rings once, then: *"Hi, this is Max. Leave me a message."*

"Hey, it's me. Where are you? I'm at the restaurant. Call me or text me or something, okay?" I say.

I set my phone down on the table, right next to my napkin, so I can keep a close eye on it. I try to read the menu, but the words kind of blur into each other.

I'm worried. Really worried. Max would never blow me off for our belated Valentine's Day date.

Another five minutes pass. Then ten. It's obvious he isn't coming, but he hasn't called or texted. Something must have happened to him. I apologize to the nice Hungarian woman, give her money for my Coke, and rush out into the snowy night.

I walk around the campus for the next half hour or so, searching for Max. I try the Chapin lobby, the library, Lanyon Hall. No success. And he still isn't responding to my calls or texts.

Maybe he had another migraine and was in too much pain to crawl out of bed. But if that were the case, Franklin would have let me know, right?

I'm trying desperately not to panic.

Eventually, I decide to go back to Kerrith to change into warmer clothes so I can hike out to the cliff. I make a mental note to grab a flashlight, too. I know there's like a zero percent chance Max is out there. But it's worth a try.

I'm calling his number again when I reach the third-floor landing. When I get to the room, a cell phone is ringing and strange noises are coming from inside.

Confused, I hang up and press my ear to the door. Is Devon crying? What's going on?

I open the door. "Devon? Are you—"

I stop in my tracks.

Devon is in my bed. Half naked. On top of Max.

37.

DEVON LEAPS TO HER FEET AND STARES AT ME WITH A HORRIFIED expression. She's wearing a white lace bra and matching thong and nothing else.

"Tess! You weren't supposed to—ohmigosh, I'm so, so sorry!" she cries out. "I feel so guilty. I never meant for this to happen."

There is a vodka bottle on my nightstand and two Thorn Abbey coffee mugs. One of them has a shimmery pink lipstick stain on it.

I stand there, frozen, unable to react. Or think. Or feel. Devon and Max? How is this possible? He *hates* her. Or that's what he told me, anyway.

A voice echoes in my head: *He's just like every other guy.*

I grit my teeth. He's *not*. I know he's not. I also know that he cares about me and would never do this to me. Something doesn't add up.

Max is lying on my bed in a pair of black boxers; the rest of his clothes are in a heap on the floor, next to a bouquet of crushed red tulips. Were they for me? His eyes are closed, and he's not moving.

"Max?" I call out.

He doesn't respond.

"Max?" I repeat, more loudly.

Still nothing.

I hurry over to him and shake him. He's out cold.

"He's kind of had a lot to drink," Devon explains sheepishly. "I feel like such a terrible person! You're never going to forgive me, are you?"

I turn to the nightstand. The bottle of vodka is almost full.

And then I notice something else. There is a brown prescription bottle and pills scattered across the floor.

I pick up the bottle and read the label. It's one of Devon's medications.

"You drugged him, didn't you?" I say slowly. "You put some of these in his drink."

"What? Ohmigosh, I would never do that!"

"If I went online right now and looked up the overdose

symptoms of this medicine, would one of them be uncon-
sciousness?"

Her eyes flash with a strange expression. Fear? Panic? Rage?
"Tess, you're imagining things. Look, I know you're upset that
we were making out. I don't blame you. But I would never do
something like that to Maxi!"

"How many pills did you give him?"

She plucks a pair of jeans and a white T-shirt from the
floor and pulls them on. "*He* initiated this meet-up," she says
stubbornly.

"*I said, how many pills did you give him?*"

"He told me he needed to talk about something important.
In private. So I told him to come up here. He was so nervous, I
offered him a drink. Maybe he'd been drinking before, I don't
know. Anyway, I had a couple of drinks too, and we both got
pretty woozy. Then all of a sudden he's kissing me and tearing
my clothes off and . . . well, you know the rest."

I knot my fists. "You goddamned bitch. I'm calling 911 and
campus security right now. And don't bother blaming your recent
'trauma' for what happened here. Because everyone will be able
to see you for exactly what you are—a lying, conniving whore!"

Devon's mouth twists into a cold, creepy smile. "You think
you're so clever, don't you? Well, you're not. You have *no* idea
who you're up against," she purrs.

"*Excuse* me?"

Max stirs. "Tess? Is that you?" he murmurs weakly.

I rush over and kneel down beside him. "Yes, it's me! How are you feeling?"

He rubs his forehead. "W-what's going on? Where am I?"

"You're in my room. Are you okay? I was just about to call 911 and get you some help."

The door slams. I turn around. Devon is gone.

Max reaches for my hand and grips it with surprising strength. "No, don't!"

"Don't what?"

"Don't call 911. Don't call anyone."

"Max, what are you talking about?"

"Tess, she knows."

"Knows what?"

Max closes his eyes wearily. "There's something I haven't told you."

38.

On Sunday, I sit on a wooden bench outside Headmaster Henle's office. Franklin is next to me, trying to keep me calm. And not succeeding. My knees won't stop shaking, and I've bitten practically all my fingernails down to the quick.

Last night, Max told me that Devon had blackmailed him into meeting her in our room. He said he would explain everything when he was more alert. I called Franklin to help me sneak Max out of Kerrith and get him back to Chapin.

But by this morning, it was too late. Devon went to the police and made some sort of accusation against Max. He's in the headmaster's office with the police now. Franklin and I are waiting for him to come out.

"*What* is going on in there?" I ask Franklin, trying to keep the hysteria out of my voice.

Franklin squeezes my hand. "Don't worry, Tess. It's just a formality."

"*What's* just a formality? What did she say to the police, anyway?"

"So I guess Max hasn't told you?"

"We haven't spoken since last night. Told me what?"

Franklin takes a deep breath. "Devon claims she has evidence that Max killed Becca."

I gasp. *"What?"*

"She claims she saw something that night, and . . ." Franklin shrugs. "Obviously, she's crazy."

"Well, yes! Obviously! Max is innocent! Besides, why now? Why didn't she go to the police last May if she suspected something?"

"Exactly."

"So they'll just question Max and that'll be it, right? Case closed?"

Franklin glances over his shoulder at the headmaster's door. "I'm not sure," he says after a moment. "I hope so. But I guess there's always a chance they'll reopen the investigation."

"*No!*" I practically shout.

"Tess. Please. We need to figure out how to help Max."

"Okay, okay."

I slump back in my seat and gnaw on my thumbnail some more. From across the hallway, Aurora Thorn's portrait stares down at me. I wish I had a tarp to cover it—or better yet, a can of black spray paint or an X-Acto knife. Not that Aurora Thorn ever did anything to me, but still . . .

Focus, I tell myself.

Devon was a pathological liar *before* her accident. And *after* her accident, she became forgetful. Kinder. Gentler. That is, until she decided to drug Max and seduce him and then go to the police with a vicious made-up story to incriminate him.

She knows.

There's something I haven't told you.

What did Max mean? What does Devon know? And what hasn't Max told me?

A few minutes later, the door opens. Franklin and I both stand. Headmaster Henle pokes his head out and motions to Franklin. "Mr. Chase, I was just about to call you. Officer Phibbs would like to speak to you. Could you go down to Dean Sanchez's office and make yourself comfortable? Officer Phibbs will be right there."

"Of course, sir."

"Miss Szekeres, this may take a few hours."

A few hours? "Um, yes, sir. I'll just head back to my dorm, then."

As I walk by the open doorway, I glance past the head-master and catch a brief glimpse of Max. A man in a fancy gray suit is leaning over and whispering something in his ear. It looks like a scene from one of the *Law & Order* episodes Mom and I used to watch.

His lawyer. That must be his lawyer.

Max really *is* in trouble.

When I get back to Kerrith, Devon is not in our room. I haven't seen her since she took off last night, although she did text me at, like, one a.m. to say that she was sleeping elsewhere, so would I please not bother sending out the bloodhounds, blah, blah, blah.

I lock the door and get to work. Devon claims that she has evidence that Max killed Becca. I'm totally, one hundred percent positive she's lying through her teeth. But maybe she fabricated something, and if so, maybe she's hiding this alleged "evidence" in our room.

I need to do a thorough and complete search, *Law & Order* style.

I start with Devon's closet. It used to be an unholy mess: piles of expensive designer clothes crumpled on the floor, mis-matched shoes scattered like bowling pins. Now it's absolutely pristine—every item hung up on padded satin hangers or lined up on the shelves. Weird. But, whatever. Maybe Devon decided to become a neat freak after her close brush with death. Or maybe she was just bored.

Working quickly, I go through pockets, sleeves, hems, shoes, shoe boxes, storage cartons. Everything smells like Becca's perfume. Ugh. I try not to think about the Valentine's Day dance; I can't afford to plunge into a deep depression right now.

After half an hour in the closet, I turn up nothing. I try her dresser. Then her bed. Then under her bed. Her nightstand.

Still nothing.

Devon's laptop is on her desk, in sleep mode. I wake it up, and a fire prevention article appears on the screen. I scan it quickly. It's incredibly technical. Is she writing a paper for chem?

Her other files and documents all seem to be school-related. And I don't have her password, so I can't access her e-mail. *Crap.*

A piece of pink paper sticks out from under the laptop with BIKEMANIA 24 FRONT ST scribbled on it. Devon on a bicycle? She told me once that her preferred modes of transportation were "business class" or "the passenger seat of a hot guy's Porsche." Her words.

I comb the rest of her desk, saving the bottom drawer for last. I guess there's a chance she stashed her "evidence" in the silver box. I open the drawer. And do a double take. Becca's red leather diary is on top of the silver box, not in it. I try the lid. It's not locked.

Strange.

I pick up the diary and flip to a random page. I haven't taken a peek since last fall. Fortunately, the thought of reading Becca's private revelations no longer makes me want to curl up and die. I know now that Max didn't love her. She's not my competition, and she never was.

March 3

I can't meet up with M tonight b/c MX's parents are in town and I have to have dinner with them. So boring. I'll have to make it up to M. I bought a little something at La Perla he's going to love love love. ☺

My breath catches in my throat. "M" isn't Max. It's someone else. Becca was hooking up with another person behind Max's back.

I think about the diary entries I read last fall. Maybe *that* "M" wasn't Max, either?

I flip through more pages. An entry from last April catches my eye:

MX is driving me crazy. Today he started to have that talk with me again, about how maybe we need to take a break or some bullshit. I pretended to cry and he backed off. Why doesn't he fall madly in love with me like everyone else? One of these days he will, and that's when I'll dump his sorry ass. Let him see what it feels like to be rejected. JERK. He is NOT allowed to humiliate me. I won't let him. He has no idea who he's up against.

At least I have M. Dear, obedient Monty. I can count on him for THAT whenever the urge strikes. We're like friends with benefits, but even better.

Oh. So M is someone named Monty. Monty who? I flip back to the pages I read last fall.

Speaking of M, he texted tonight and said he wants to meet up this weekend. I don't know what to tell him. I want to be with him, but I know I shouldn't. I'm so mixed up.

Last night, D spent the night down the hall, and M spent the night in our room. Heaven.

And then it hits me.

Monty—"M"—is Killian Montgomery. I remember him telling me ages ago that he and Becca had nicknames for each other. She was his "Becky." He must have been her "Monty."

Becca was cheating on Max with Killian. With her cousin.

39.

I SINK DOWN TO THE FLOOR, SHAKING MY HEAD IN DISBELIEF. Becca was hooking up with Killian, just for the sex? How long had that been going on? Did Max ever suspect?

I should have known. Max said he and Becca only dated for a few months before she died. She was writing about hooking up with "M" way back in September of the previous year.

I text both Max and Franklin to contact me *the second* their meetings are over.

I need to read more of Becca's diary. I want to figure out what, if anything, Becca's relationship with Killian had to do with whatever it is Devon knows about her death . . . or *thinks* she knows . . . or is *pretending* she knows.

There are so many layers to this mystery. My head is spinning, and the stress is making me hungry. I get up and grab an emergency snack from my desk—sour cream and onion chips and Double Stuf Oreos—and hunker down with the diary.

April 6

Can you believe W thought I would actually attend her birthday party? Why would I want to spend the weekend with her at her family's little shack in Truro? I would DIE of boredom with her and the other Drama Club kids. And my lips would fall off from fake smiling for 48 straight hours.

It's funny—W always says I'm so sweet. On the outside, I am. I have to be. Otherwise, people might start to hate me. And THEN what?

April 15

C wrote my T. S. Eliot paper for me. He thinks I'm going to break up with MX for him haha.

April 22

I actually got F to cover for me with MX when M and I had our meet-up Saturday. It didn't take much to convince F. Poor thing, I think he has a crush on me.

April 24

I've got it all figured it out with MX. He gets mad when I flirt with other boys. But if I beg him for forgiveness, he's placated. At least for a while. I do like him. Sometimes I think I could even fall in love with him. But I don't believe in love, and besides, he's not enough for me. I'm not sure if anyone is.

April 28

No boys around. MX and M are both out of town. It's probably just as well because I'm feeling really fat and ugly this weekend. I need someone to remind me I'm beautiful.

Deep down I'm just like any other girl, I suppose. A bottomless pit of insecurity. So unattractive.

I need a fucking drink.

May 1

I feel a little guilty. D idolizes me. She also seems to idolize the idea of me and MX together. Like we're some fairy-tale couple. Like we're William and Kate.

I wonder if D suspects about M. That it's not MX I'm actually sneaking into our room on weekends.

266

Wait, *what*? Devon told me that Becca used to sneak Max into their room. But it was actually Killian all along? Did Devon know?

I skip ahead to the very end. What was going on between Becca and Max and Killian right before she died?

I flip to the final entry.

It's not from last May.

It's from a few days ago. February 20, to be exact.

Fuck him. FUCK HIM!!!!!! He forced my hand, telling his stupid little girlfriend the truth. Well, his version of the truth, anyway. How DARE he say those things about me?

This is all his fault. HIS FAULT. Besides, D stopped listening and obeying. She's been way too nice, too forgiving. What, is that pathetic poser her new BFF now? I warned her about that.

I don't know if it was the meds or what. I should have made her stop taking them way sooner. In any case, I lost her. She was lost. I had to lead her to the cliff. She had to die. People have to know what really happened last spring.

She had to die? *Who* had to die?

This is beyond freaky. Frowning, I read the entry once,

twice, three times. The handwriting is almost but not quite the same as the handwriting in the rest of the diary.

What the hell? Did Devon have a total psychotic break-down? Does she believe on some unconscious level that she's Becca?

Did *she* kill Becca? But the timing doesn't work.

I lean back in my chair and munch on an Oreo and think about when I first met Devon. And all the creepy things that started happening when I arrived at Thorn Abbey. The mysterious crying from Gita's room next door. Devon's sleep-talking spells in the middle of the night.

Soon after that, me getting injured on the Kerrith stairs. The glowing seagull. The burning-hot inscription in Max's book of love poems. The flying ember at the Corn Roast. The bloodred message on the wall above my bed. The lounge vandalization.

And all the rest of it too: tapping noises on the ceiling, temperature changes, more sleep-talking.

I think about last Tuesday, when we found Devon's lifeless body on the beach. She was dead. She was absolutely, positively dead. I'm sure of it.

When she got home from the hospital, she was so chipper and cheerful at first. She acted so sweet around her mom. The same person Devon routinely called "a psychotic bitch" and "an annoying whore."

If you met her, you'd think she was the sweetest, kindest, most together girl.

Then she drugged Max and tried to have sex with him.

And turned him in to the police.

It was all an act.

She was the worst thing that ever happened to me.

I bolt straight up.

Oh my God.

Devon doesn't *think* she's Becca.

Devon *is* Becca.

40.

AT A QUARTER TILL FIVE, I FINALLY GET A TEXT FROM MAX.

It's over. All is well. Meet me at the assembly at five and I'll tell you everything.

Assembly? At five? And then I remember. There is a special Founder's Assembly in Lanyon Hall, commemorating the founding of Thorn Abbey.

Despite the fact that I'm freaking out and hyperventilating and basically losing my mind, I manage to remember that I'm supposed to be in dress uniform for this event. I peel off my jeans and hoodie and throw on my white blouse, plaid skirt, navy blazer, and tights. I glance in the mirror. My skirt is inside out. My tights have a big hole in them. Cursing in frustration,

I ransack my dresser for a new pair of tights while I balance on one leg and peel off my skirt.

I have to take a deep breath and chill.

But how can I?

Becca never died. Not really. As far as I can piece together, her spirit lived on even after her body was gone and messed with me . . . and Max? . . . and other people too? . . . all these months.

I should have listened to Kayleigh. Thorn Abbey *is* haunted. And now Devon, or the person who used to be Devon, is possessed by Becca's ghost. Or demon. Or whatever.

I peer nervously around the room. Is Devon/Becca here right now? Can she turn invisible? Slink into walls and ceilings? Read minds? I have no idea how paranormal creatures operate or what superpowers they have, if any.

I have to get out of here, like, *now*. I don't want to be alone.

And I have to tell Max right away. We need to find Devon/Becca and stop her somehow before she does any more damage.

That is, if Max will believe my demented story. I barely believe it myself.

Once inside Lanyon Hall, I sprint all the way to the main auditorium in my good shoes. Or what Devon used to call my "knockoffs of discount shoes pretending to be knockoffs," back in her super-bitchy days.

I brush back a tear. I can't believe Devon is actually dead. She wasn't a saint. Far from it. But she didn't deserve to have her life taken by an evil succubus who used to be her best friend.

As I run, I try Max on his cell several times, but the calls keep failing. Reception in Lanyon is spotty. I heard the school is planning to renovate the building next year. Hopefully, there will be real coverage then. It's after five, so the halls are pretty much empty except for me and a couple of other latecomers, including Mila Kunis.

"Hey, Tess. Where's the fire?" she jokes.

I smile grimly at her and hurry my steps.

Outside the auditorium, I pull open one of the double doors and hold it for Mila Kunis. A few others slip in too. The door closes behind me, and a faint clang sounds above the din of everyone talking.

The room is packed with students, teachers, and administrators. On the stage, Headmaster Henle fiddles with the microphone; he taps it and turns it on and off while behind him a panel of speakers sip water and wait patiently.

I spot Max in one of the back rows. He cranes his neck and waves me over. I see Franklin on the other side of the aisle, and

Yoonie, Elinor, and Priscilla, too. Killian is up front. But I don't see Devon/Becca anywhere.

I scoot into the seat next to Max. He smiles wearily and wraps his arm around my shoulders. "I'm so glad to see you," he murmurs.

His hair is rumpled, and there are black circles under his eyes, like he hasn't slept in days. My heart aches for him. He's been through so much these past twenty-four hours.

And now I'm about to tell him the worst part.

I take a deep breath. "Max. We have to talk."

"I know, I know," Max says hastily. "I'm really sorry about what happened yesterday. And today, too. The meeting went on forever, and it was a fucking nightmare. My parents are in Hong Kong on business, so they had our family lawyer fly up from the city to represent me."

"But, Max—"

"No, it's okay. Everything's fine now. It's complicated. This morning, Devon went to the police and told them that she saw me kill Becca, the night she died. But Franklin gave me an alibi, so I've been cleared."

Franklin gave me an alibi. What alibi? Max didn't mention Franklin when he told me about that awful night with Becca.

But we don't have time to get into that now. "That's great news," I say, giving him a quick hug. "I'm glad you're okay. But that's not all I wanted to talk to you about. I've figured it out. Devon isn't Devon. She's Becca."

Max looks at me like I'm a total lunatic.

Microphone feedback screeches over the speakers. "Okay, well, now that we've got this puppy working . . . welcome to our annual Founder's Assembly!" Headmaster Henle says loudly.

Everyone claps politely.

"Before I introduce our speakers, I want to say a few words about what Thorn Abbey means to me, both as a physical and nonphysical entity," he goes on.

Max leans toward me. "You're joking, right?" he whispers.

"The physical entity, of course, is what we owe to the generosity and long-range vision of the late, great Mr. Augustus Thorn. The nonphysical entity is the rest of it: our mission, our curriculum, our high standards."

"I know it sounds insane. But the person you *think* is Devon is actually Becca in Devon's body," I whisper back to Max.

The precalc teacher, Mr. Millstein, twists around in his seat. "No talking, please," he says sternly.

"Sorry, sir," Max apologizes. He turns to me and mouths: *What?*

Frustrated, I pull out my cell phone and start composing a text:

B's ghost or whatever has been haunting Thorn Abbey. She tried to keep us apart and break us up. She also tried to make my life miserable. Sometimes she used D to help her.

Last Mon. you told me you never loved B and said those other things about her. I think that made her really mad. So she killed D and took over her body.

I'm afraid of what she might do next.

I pass my phone to Max.

As he reads, the color drains from his face.

"On this day in 1875, Augustus Thorn gifted his magnificent estate to our school," Headmaster Henle says, sweeping his arms in a wide circle.

Just then, I notice a strange smell. A burning smell.

Max shoves my phone at me.

HOW DO YOU KNOW ALL THIS??????

I type back:

Too much to explain now. I read B's old diary. It was in D's desk. There was a new entry from last Thurs. The day "Devon" came back from the hospital. B wrote that D had to die because she wasn't obeying anymore. She wrote that people had to know what really happened last spring, whatever that means?

Max reads my text intently. And shakes his head. And keeps shaking his head.

"No," he whispers. "No, no, no."

He looks as though he might start crying. I stroke his arm. It can't be easy for him to learn that his dead ex-girlfriend is a murderer. Also, that she's not exactly dead.

The burning smell is stronger now. A few seats over, a girl sniffs and asks, "Is that smoke?"

Several people point to the ceiling. I glance up. A thin ribbon of black curls out from under one of the fluorescent lights. More smoke snakes out from the overhead air vents.

"Fire!" someone yells.

Pandemonium ensues. People scream and scramble out of their seats. I snatch my phone from Max and try to call 911, but there's still no signal. No one else around us has service either.

"The sprinklers should go off any second," one of the teachers shouts nearby, trying to calm us.

"Tess! This way!" Max grabs my hand and practically drags me to the exit closest to us. He and I push at the double doors. They open slightly, then jam. Through the thin crack between the doors, I can just make out an orange lock, like for a bike, dangling from a chain.

Frantic, I glance around at the three other sets of double doors. People are pushing them, pounding their fists, shouting for help.

Oh my God. Someone has barricaded all four exits and set the place on fire.

Becca.

I cover my eyes with my hands and squint up at the ceiling. The smoke pouring out of the lighting fixtures and air vents is thicker and heavier now. Brown stains bloom and bubble across the white acoustic tiles, and the metal frames around them sag and crumple. Becca must have started the fire in the attic, or whatever's above the drop ceiling.

"Please stay calm!" Headmaster Henle's voice booms over the speakers. "Starting with the first row, please form an orderly line, make your way up the center aisle, and come up to the stage. There's an emergency exit behind these curtains."

More pandemonium. Everyone rushes to the front of the auditorium. The smoke swells and spreads and slowly banks down. It hovers a few feet above our heads like an ominous cloud.

Max tugs on my arm. "Tess, come on. We need to go!"

"Okay, okay!"

We join the mob storming toward the stage. My eyes sting and burn. Max coughs. The smoke continues to descend.

"Are you okay?" I gasp.

"Yeah, are you?" he asks.

A piece of acoustic tile comes crashing down, spitting flame. The drop ceiling is breaking up. Through the smoke, I can make out a light fixture dangling precariously on a wire.

More screams, more chaos, more showering debris. A small fire sizzles and spreads across the carpet.

"Tess, look out!" Max yells.

I feel his strong arms grab me from behind. At the same moment, Becca's face flashes in my vision. "It's your turn to die, bitch," she says, laughing shrilly.

And then . . . darkness.

41.

THIS TIME, THE DREAM IS DIFFERENT. MAX AND I ARE TOGETHER. He is lying next to me, and we are holding hands. I'm not sure where we are—maybe in Hunters' Meadow, maybe on the beach. The sun is blazing down on us, and when I close my eyes, I see white. His body is warm and familiar against mine. I feel peaceful, content.

But something is obviously bothering him.

"What is it? What's wrong?" I ask him.

"I'm so sorry, Tess."

"Sorry for what?"

"I would have told you before. But I was afraid you'd hate me."

I sit up and gaze down at him serenely. "Max! I could never, ever hate you."

He sits up too and cradles my face with his hand. "I wish that were true. But it doesn't matter now. I need to tell you everything. Before it's too late."

"Tell me what? Before *what's* too late?"

He looks away. "I killed Becca."

I smile and trail my finger down the jagged scar on his cheek. "Uh-huh."

"No . . . *listen!* That night, she and I took a walk. To the beach. I told her that I wanted to break up."

I stop smiling. He isn't joking.

This dream is getting really weird.

"At first she tried to talk me out of it. She cried and begged," Max says. "But I told her I was sure this time."

"And?"

"She was furious," he goes on. "She screamed at me, practically frothing at the mouth. I'd never seen her like that. Then she laughed at me. She said I was a stupid idiot . . . that she'd been getting with Killian behind my back the entire time we were together."

"Her cousin Killian?" I say, as if I didn't know.

"Yes, her cousin Killian. Anyway, by then we'd reached the cliff. When she told me the thing about Killian, I called her some pretty awful names and told her I never wanted to see her face again. She grabbed my arm and wouldn't let go.

We struggled, and next thing I knew, she went over the side of the cliff."

"Oh my God!"

"It was horrible. The thing is, I have no idea if she fell by accident or if I pushed her or what. I ran down to the water to look for her. But I couldn't find her."

He is talking faster and faster now; the dream is speeding up.

"I should have just gone to the police and told them the truth. But I was scared they'd throw me in jail forever. So I did the dumbest thing I ever did. I covered it up. I took her favorite sailboat from the school marina and let it float out to sea. There was a storm later that night, so everyone figured her boat capsized and she drowned."

"Oh, Max."

I start to cry. I can't stand the thought of him in so much pain.

But this is just a dream. *My* dream. I can help him.

Max wipes my tears away. "You hate me now, right?"

"No, I don't hate you. What happened is in the past. You need to forgive yourself and let it go."

"I can't."

"Yes, you can."

"How?"

"We'll figure it out. Together."

He laces his fingers through mine. "I love you, Tess."

"I love you too, Max."

"I'll always love you." His voice sounds far away.

"I'll always love you too."

He leans over me and kisses me on the lips tenderly. So tenderly.

"Let's wake up now," I tell him.

But it's too late.

He's gone.

When I open my eyes, Max is lying next to me, clutching my hand.

"Max?" I say. But my throat burns, and my voice is a useless rasp.

I start to get up, but pain sears through my head and forces me to stay still. What happened to me?

The air is dense with smoke and unbearably hot. It smells awful, like burning plastic. It's also insanely loud. I hear flames roaring, water gushing, chain saws grinding.

Oh, right. There was a fire in the auditorium.

"Is anyone trapped?" a man shouts. He sounds weirdly amplified.

Something tickles my face. There is a heavy cloth over my

nose and mouth. I touch it. Max's school blazer. He must have put it there to protect me from the smoke.

"Thank you," I whisper, squeezing Max's hand. It hurts to move my head.

He squeezes back.

"Are you okay?" I ask.

His hand goes slack and falls away from mine.

"Max?"

To hell with the pain. I turn toward him. His eyes are closed. Blood gushes out of his head.

"MAX!"

A figure in black and bright yellow suddenly looms over us. Over Max. "We need more manpower here, *now*!" he yells.

No. This can't be happening.

I close my eyes and pray.

Please let him live.

Please let him live.

Please let him live.

42.

HE DOESN'T LIVE.

He was one of six students who didn't make it.

Max died saving my life. From what the firefighters and the medics could piece together, he pushed me out of the path of a falling light fixture. It landed on him instead, and he suffered massive internal and external injuries. He was conscious long enough to put his blazer over my nose and mouth. He died soon after.

Three students are still in intensive care. Including Franklin, who suffered brain damage and is in a coma.

The girls—Priscilla, Yoonie, and Elinor—all escaped with minor injuries, as did Killian.

In the hospital, Officer Phibbs asked me a bunch of questions about Devon. Or the person everyone *thinks* is Devon. She's missing, and the police are searching for her. She's the lead suspect in the arson.

According to Officer Phibbs, she left fingerprints on the centralized smoke detection and fire sprinkler systems when she disabled them. And she crawled through a maintenance hatch to throw gasoline-soaked rags on top of the drop ceiling. The fire grew like crazy in that confined space before anyone noticed it, at which point it was too late.

Officer Phibbs asked me if I could think of any reason my roommate tried to burn down the auditorium with all her classmates and teachers in it.

She's not my roommate, I wanted to say. *She's a demon who killed my roommate, then possessed her body.*

But I didn't have it in me to explain. He wouldn't have believed me anyway.

I just hope she's back in hell, where she belongs.

I'm ten minutes late for the memorial service for Max and the other fire victims. It took me forever to figure out what to wear. I wanted to look nice for Max.

When I realized that Max wouldn't be there, and in any

case would have teased me for obsessing about an outfit, I smiled. Then laughed. Then burst into tears. I couldn't stop sobbing for almost an hour.

I hurry toward the quad, smoothing down my navy-blue plaid skirt over my panty hose with the run in them. The service is being held there because Lanyon Hall has been closed indefinitely for renovations. Fortunately, it's pretty warm out for March.

After the fire, Mom came and stayed with me for ten days. At first, I couldn't eat or sleep. I couldn't do anything but lie in bed in a fetal position. The doctor prescribed some medication for me, though. And now I'm able to function. Sort of. Barely.

Mom had planned to return for the service, but she came down with the flu and had to cancel. She's left me half a dozen messages on my phone in her croaky flu voice, asking me if I'm okay and telling me how much she loves me.

When I get to the quad, Yoonie and her chamber group are playing that uplifting Bach piece people always play at funerals. Headmaster Henle, Dean Sanchez, a priest, a minister, and a rabbi are standing up front, their heads bent respectfully.

I look around for a place to sit. There are hundreds of people there, weeping and passing around Kleenexes. I spot Elinor and Priscilla holding hands in the back, dressed in identical black suits and sunglasses. Killian is with his lacrosse friends.

For a moment, I consider returning to Kerrith. Or walking through the woods to *The Eternal Spirit*, where Augustus and Aurora Thorn are buried . . . where Max and I first kissed. I don't belong here. This isn't where I want to mourn for him. I would rather be alone with my memories. My grief feels too private, too boundless, to share with a crowd.

Then I spot Mr. and Mrs. De Villiers in the front row. I can't see their faces, but I know it's them. I recognize his big shoulders, which are so like Max's, and her glossy auburn hair.

I take a deep breath and walk over to them.

Mr. De Villiers glances up at me. He looks ten years older than the last time I saw him. "Why, hello, Tess," he says with a frail smile.

Mrs. De Villiers dabs at her eyes with a white silk handkerchief. Then she pats the empty seat next to her.

Surprised, I sit down. She takes my hand in hers.

"Max spoke of you often," she says quietly. "You made him very happy."

I start crying again.

She starts crying too. We bend our heads together, grieving.

That night, I sit on the cliff gazing out at the sea, which is very still and black. For some strange reason, I feel close to Max here tonight.

I think about my mom's mom, who passed away a couple of years ago. Mom claims that Grandma comes to her in her dreams and talks to her. She also claims that Grandma saved her life once by warning her not to take I-87 to work that particular morning. Mom went on a back road instead; she got yelled at by her boss for being late. Later, she heard on the radio that a tractor-trailer had jackknifed on the highway near the Avery Park exit and that three people had died.

I never used to believe Mom about any of this stuff. But now I do. People's spirits do live on after they pass away. Good spirits and bad spirits. I think that Kayleigh was right about everything that happened at Thorn Abbey after all.

Maybe I *should* get a cat's-eye or peridot amulet, for protection.

I hug my knees to my chest and look up at the sky. I try to make out the Big Dipper, Orion, the Pleiades.

I wonder if Max is a star now. Or an asterism.

I wonder if he'll keep talking to me in my dreams for the rest of my life.

I hope so.

EPILOGUE

I CARRY THE LAST OF MY BOXES ACROSS THE PARKING LOT AND put it in the back of Mom's old Volvo station wagon. I can't believe I've accumulated so much stuff in the nine months I've been at Thorn Abbey—books, notebooks, and, of course, my coveted trophy from the end-of-the-year student banquet: "Most Likely to Win a Pulitzer Prize."

"Is that it, honey bunny?" my mom asks me. She wipes the sweat from her brow and smiles cheerfully at me, although I can tell she's exhausted from the heat and the long drive from Avery Park.

"I think so. I just want to take a final look around."

"No problem. I'm going to get myself some water, and I'll wait for you here. Maybe I'll even bond with the other parents."

"Thanks, Mom."

I grab an empty garbage bag from the backseat in case there's anything left in the room and start the trek back to Kerrith Hall. The quad is beautiful—lush grass, flowers in full bloom, sunlight glistening on the spray from the fountain. In my mind, I don't even think of it as "Becca's fountain" anymore. I pass dozens of now-familiar faces, everyone lugging boxes, dragging suitcases, saying their good-byes.

I think about all the times I wanted to leave this place. Including just after the fire. I'm glad I hung in there, somehow. And I'm glad I'm coming back in the fall.

It's been over three months since Max passed away. Things are starting to feel a little bit normal again. I've been visiting *The Eternal Spirit* every week and talking to Max. Telling him about my classes, the girls, my new favorite potato chips, whatever. Each week has been getting easier and easier. These last few times, I've managed to get through the entire visit without crying. Or crying much, anyway.

As I cross the quad, I run into Yoonie. We exchange hugs and promise to stay in touch over the summer.

"Listen, I think we should totally room together next year," she adds.

I smile, pleased that Yoonie suggested this. Since the fire and Devon's disappearance, the dynamic of our group has shifted somewhat. All the girls are nicer to me. Especially Yoonie.

"What about Elinor and Priscilla?" I point out.

"They can double up next door. I'm hella sick of their snoring."

I laugh. "Okay, then."

"When you get your roommate request form in the mail next month, just put my name down. I'll put yours."

"Great."

"Oh, and didn't you say you played oboe at your old school?"

"Clarinet," I correct her.

"Same difference. Bring your instrument in September. The music department's trying to put together a wind ensemble."

I try to visualize playing the clarinet at Thorn Abbey. It's a cool idea, and I'd probably make a whole new group of friends. "Sounds good. Thanks. Have a nice summer, Yoonie."

"You too, roomie."

We exchange one final hug, and I continue on toward Kerrith.

"Tess!"

Killian saunters up to me.

"Hello, my love," he says, kissing me on both cheeks. "I haven't seen you in ages. I hope you weren't planning on leaving without saying good-bye."

I hesitate. After the fire, Killian sent me a note expressing his condolences. I sent him a short thank-you e-mail, but other than that, I've been avoiding him.

It might be irrational, but deep down, I associate Killian with the chain of events culminating in Max's death. Killian and Becca were cousins who hooked up for hot sex. Becca told Max about her and Killian on that fateful night when Max tried to break up with her for good.

Which led to Becca's death.

Which led to Becca turning into a vengeful demon.

Which led to the fire.

Which led to Max's death.

Killian smiles a little too brightly. "So! What are you doing this summer? Are you going to come visit me in Philly so I can show you around?"

"I'm taking some classes at the University at Albany, so I'll be pretty tied up," I reply.

"My goodness, we're ambitious! Well, if you change your mind, you know where to find me."

I gaze into his Abercrombie-model blue eyes. He is ridiculously handsome. And charming. And amoral.

"See you in the fall, Killian," I say finally.

"Yes, see you in the fall, darling."

I wave and walk away.

All of a sudden, I can't wait to leave this complicated, drama-filled place and go home to Avery Park. To the little tan ranch with the scrubby, overgrown lawn. To the strip malls with the cheap nail salons. To *Law & Order* on Friday nights. To Kayleigh and ice-cream binges.

I'm sure the feeling will wear off in a couple of weeks. I'm not the same person I was when I first came to Thorn Abbey.

But still.

As I near the north end of the quad, I can just make out a boy sitting on the steps of Kerrith. His face is turned away from me. I flash back to October, when Max sat at the very same spot, waiting for me as I stumbled home from Killian's party, wasted out of my mind.

Max. Oh, Max.

The boy on the steps rises to his feet slowly, with the help of a cane. I realize with a start that it's Franklin.

"Hey!" I run up to him and give him a big hug. "What are you doing here? Why aren't you in New York?"

"I decided to play hooky. I wanted to come up and visit before everyone was gone for the summer."

"Oh, wow. I'm incredibly glad to see you."

"I'm glad to see you, too."

After the fire, Franklin was in a coma for two and a half

months. Max's father convinced Franklin's parents to have him transported to some fancy, high-tech hospital in New York City at the De Villierses' expense.

One day, Franklin's vitals spiraled out of control and he almost died. The next day, he woke up and asked for a glass of orange juice as if nothing had happened. Just like that. The doctors had no explanation for his sudden recovery. They called him "the miracle patient."

"You didn't drive all the way up here by yourself, did you?" I ask him, concerned.

"My d—that is, Mr. De Villiers, insisted on playing chauffeur. He has this new Bentley SUV he wanted to test out. The guy's obsessed with cars."

"Yeah, I remember."

We stand in silence for a long moment. There's so much to talk about. And yet neither of us seems to want to go there.

"Well," we both say at the same time.

We laugh, a little uncomfortably.

"I guess I'd better be going." I glance over my shoulder. "My mom's waiting for me in the parking lot, and she's pretty much wilting from the heat. Maybe I'll visit you in the city this summer?"

"I'd like that. Hey, Tess? Before you go?"

"What?"

"There's something I haven't told you," he says.

Franklin leans in so that we are just inches apart. He reaches out and cradles my face with his hand. The way *he* used to.

I stare at him in shock.

He cracks a smile. A ghost of a smile.

I stifle a scream.

ACKNOWLEDGMENTS

Thank you . . .

To my editor, Annette Pollert, for being brilliant, thoughtful, and just plain wonderful.

To the rest of the amazing Simon Pulse team, including Bethany Buck, Mara Anastas, Jennifer Klonsky, Lucille Rettino, Julie Christopher, Carolyn Swerdloff, Emma Sector, Paul Crichton, Anna McKean, Katherine Devendorf, Karen Taschek, Christina Bryza, Brian Luster, Susan Goldfarb, Sara Berko, Angela Goddard, Mary Marotta, Christina Pecorale, Maria Faria, Brian Kelleher, Jim Conlin, Theresa Brumm, and Victor Iannone.

To my agents, Lydia Wills and Nora Spiegel, for absolutely everything. You two are the best.

To Jeremy Rodd for teaching me about fires. I am in awe of the work you and other firefighters do for the rest of us every day.

To Christopher Reynolds, who read the manuscript and offered spot-on suggestions.

To Amy Desmond, Eileen Gilbert, Gwen Guarino, Cindy Litts, Mari MacLean, Carol Ohlin, Marice Pappo, Stephanie Raney, and Elaine Rodd for being there for my family and me so I could immerse myself in the world of Tess, Max, Becca, and Devon.

To Jens, Christopher, and Clara. You guys are my heart and soul, always and forever.

And last but not least, to the late, great Daphne du Maurier for inspiring me to write *Always, Forever*.

1

QUEEN VEDA, THE SECOND MONARCH OF THE ROYAL KINGDOM of Ran, stood inside her enormous wardrobe and surveyed the contents.

Her dresses were organized by occasion. On the left were the ones for affairs of state. Next to them, evening clothes. Then day clothes, then hunting clothes, then clothes for brisk exercise.

The dresses on the far right were for funerals and executions. She took one of them off its hanger and examined it. It was a long, wonderfully soft gown made out of black velvet. The collar was pure fawn, and the buttons, onyx inlaid with rubies.

The queen held the gown up to her body. The onyx was the color of her long, shiny black hair; the rubies were the color of her lips. She ran her fingers over the fawn collar.

She turned to the Beauty Consultant, who was sitting on his favorite stool. He was plucking apart a long-stemmed red rose.

"Well?" she demanded.

But the Beauty Consultant was engrossed in his rose. He was a tiny man, no taller than her dressing table. He had a shriveled bald head and hooded black eyes. The queen was not sure how old he was—perhaps a hundred, perhaps older. She had inherited him from her mother, the Lady Despina.

Momi. God rest her soul, she thought.

Or maybe not.

The Beauty Consultant was still absorbed in dismembering the rose. There were red petals scattered all over his lap.

"Well?" the queen repeated, irritated.

The Beauty Consultant barely raised his head. He regarded the queen. His hooded black eyes glowed silver for a moment, then turned bright green. The queen smiled a slow, satisfied smile. The colors never lied.

"Yes, Majesty, most becoming," the Beauty Consultant whispered. He held the nearly beheaded red rose up to his mouth and nibbled delicately on a thorn.

Queen Veda returned the black velvet dress to its hanger, stroking the collar one last time. When was the last time she had worn this dress? Oh, yes. Galen's funeral. And just before that, at the funeral of Galen's young friend, Jana or Jaffa or whatever.

"The pink one, Your Majesty!" the Beauty Consultant whispered, startling her.

The pink one. Queen Veda ran her fingertips across her dresses, searching for it. All her dresses were lined up neat as soldiers: black silk with gold brocade, brown taffeta, emerald-green satin, red mohair with matching cape.

Ah, there it was. The pink lace gown was the only item of pink clothing she owned. It was a daring shade for her to wear, at her advanced age of— Anyhow, it was a pale, delicate pink, the color of a young girl's blushing cheeks. It was a color she herself used to favor as a young girl. Galen had liked it on her, and of course, before Galen, the other ones.

Queen Veda held it up to her body. The lace was so delicate: wisps of pink thread engaged in a gossamer geometry of flowers, birds, hearts.

She smiled at the Beauty Consultant, waiting for an answer. He was flinging the rose petals off his lap, one by one, and muttering in his strange language, which she had never understood:

"*Desse ciara treffen du mara.*"

"Pay attention!" the queen demanded.

The Beauty Consultant stopped muttering and stared at her. His eyes turned briefly cloudy, then settled back into their oily, inscrutable blackness. The Queen felt a rush of something unexpected—disappointment, rage. She gave a snort of annoyance and jammed the gown back onto its hanger.

"It was your idea," she muttered.

There was a ripping sound. One of her long fingernails had caught on the lace and torn part of the neckline.

The queen was about to extract her fingernail when she noticed that the Beauty Consultant's eyes were glowing red. Fueled by the compliment, Queen Veda continued ripping, ripping all the way down the bodice.

It was so easy. Pleasant, even.

When she was done, she was breathing hard. Her fingernails had dug into her palms, piercing the skin. But it didn't matter. The Beauty Consultant's eyes told her what she needed to know. They were the color of fire, of the fallen rose petals, of the blood that streaked her hands.

"Yes, it is you. It has always been you. And it will always be you," the Beauty Consultant whispered. "Your Majesty!"

Yes, yes, yes, she thought.

A magnificent sense of calm washed over her.

2

Princess Tatiana Anatolia, daughter of Queen Veda, sat cross-legged on her velvet window seat and stared out at the royal garden. Snow fell softly on the landscape, obscuring everything in pure white: the gnarled rosebushes, the glass conservatory, the stone fountain. The winged boy with the permanent snarl was spitting a long, thin stream of ice.

Ana, as she was called, reached down and scratched her toes. The nails on them were long and ragged. She studied their peculiar color—black, with ripples of green and yellow—and marveled at their sheer ugliness. It had taken a long time to get them that way.

"Ana."

The door inched open, and Omi entered. Her pale golden

hair was piled in high curls on her head, and the gray wool dress she wore looked wonderfully soft and cozy. *How nice it would be to curl up and sleep in it*, Ana thought. She hugged her knees and rocked back and forth.

Omi pushed the door closed with her hip. She was carrying a silver tray. "I brought you fruit."

Ana shook her head. "No, no fruit. I asked for pastries."

Omi set the tray on a table. There was a large bowl filled with apples, pomegranates, and orange blossoms. The fruit, Ana knew, had been grown in the conservatory along with the queen's winter flowers and her special beauty herbs. Next to the bowl was a curved knife and a white napkin embroidered with the queen's royal crest—a peregrine falcon, a tangled vine of roses, and the initial *V* in old Innish script.

"Child, you have been eating nothing but pastries for many moons now," Omi scolded. "You need fruit. Or else you will—"

"—grow even fatter than I am?" Ana finished.

Omi frowned. Her blue eyes, which were so pale that they looked almost transparent, regarded Ana with a mixture of anger and worry. Omi had been Ana's wet nurse when she was born. To this day, the soft almond smell of Omi's skin evoked in Ana a primal memory of feeding. The smell of her mother's skin did not have that effect on her at all.

"Tatiana Anatolia, why are you doing this to yourself? To the queen?" Omi demanded.

"Why, has she said anything?" Ana asked with interest.

"No. She hasn't. But how do you imagine this looks for her, how she must feel, having her only child neglect herself like this?"

Ana burst into laughter. "Bring me the pastries, or I will not eat anything at all."

Omi opened her mouth to say something, then clamped it shut. She turned with a sweep of her gray skirt and headed for the door.

"The cloudberry ones, and the ones with bitter chocolate!" Ana called after her. "Half a dozen of each. Or I will tell the queen you have been disobedient!"

The door closed, not gently. Ana stopped laughing.

A branch scraped against the window. The snow was falling harder now, so that the garden was all but invisible. Ana could just make out the glass walls of the conservatory and a single figure inside, moving around by lamplight.

Is it her? Or is it that nasty little man? Ana wondered.

The lamp went out. The conservatory and the person inside it blurred and faded into white.

Ana leaned back against the velvet pillows and stretched out her legs. She reached over and picked up the silver knife from the tray.

She turned it over and over again in her hand. The blade was so shiny, so perfect. She imagined peeling an apple with it and letting the skin coil into her mouth. Or slicing a pomegranate in half and exposing the slippery red seeds.

Ana used to love apples and pomegranates. She used to love orange blossoms, too, with their honey-sweet smell. Omi knew all this. But none of it could touch Ana anymore.

She ran one finger across the blade of the knife and felt the sharp, sudden sting of blood. Then she took a lock of her long golden-brown hair and ran the blade across it. Shreds of hair sprayed across her lap.

She sliced another lock, and then another, and then another. She could not see what she was doing, but that was good. Soon her hair would be as hideous as the rest of her.

3

FOUR YEARS AGO, WHEN ANA TURNED TWELVE, THE QUEEN organized a party for her, as was her annual custom. Everything about the party was lovely: the ballroom adorned with rosebushes and plumeria trees, the wild butterflies flitting through the air, the actors from Catonia performing elaborate dreamplays and shadow dances. Hundreds of dignitaries and royals were in attendance, along with the most important citizens of Ran. They drank copious amounts of wine out of silver goblets and ate tiny, perfect confections shaped like jewels.

The queen had had a red velvet dress made for the occasion, for Ana. "You are not a little girl anymore, darling Tatiana," she had said to Ana before the party as she helped her on with the dress. "You are almost a young woman."

"Yes, Momi."

"You must make me proud tonight!"

"Yes, Momi."

Out in the ballroom Ana watched her mother mingling with her guests. The queen was dressed in a green silk gown that rustled stiffly as she moved. Ana thought that she must be the most beautiful mother in the world. And the most gracious, too—she seemed to know everyone's names as well as the names of their wives, husbands, and children. "How are you, dearest Eleni? How is your darling son Maximilian? Is he still riding and playing Kings? And how is your husband enjoying his work at the Ministry?" Ana couldn't imagine such clever words coming out of her own mouth.

The trill of a bamboo flute rose and hovered in the air as the shadow dancers wove through the crowd, leaping and turning. Ana's red velvet collar itched. She picked and scratched at it. She noticed a lot of people smiling at her, though, so she stopped what she was doing and dropped her hands to her sides.

The bamboo flute grew louder and more insistent. Just then Ana spotted her mother walking up to her, the green silk of her skirt swishing and crinkling around her ankles. There was a man at her side. He was dressed in gold and black, the royal colors of Kieska.

"Darling!" The queen enfolded Ana in her arms, too tightly. Ana flinched.

"Ana, I would like you to meet Ambassador Bertl," the queen announced loudly. "Bertl, this is my daughter, Tatiana Anatolia."

Ana found herself staring at the man. He had long, curly brown hair and lovely green eyes.

"Your Excellency," Bertl murmured, bowing. Then he took Ana's hand and kissed it.

Ana's cheeks burned. She gave a little cough. "Thank you for being here," she heard herself saying mechanically. Her mother had instructed her to say that to each and every guest. "I hope you are enjoying yourself."

"Yes, yes, of course."

"Bertl, have you tried the turtle's egg canapés?" the queen trilled.

Bertl didn't respond. Ana realized, with surprise, that he was gazing at her—*her*. He seemed to be studying her as though she were a particularly fascinating plant.

"Veda, you have done well," Bertl said, finally.

"What do you mean, dear Bertl?"

"This. Your daughter. Look at her!" Bertl smiled at Ana in a way that made her blush even more deeply. "Your daughter, your little Tatiana, is going to be the greatest beauty in Ran someday. Take my word for it."

Ana's breath caught in her throat. No one had ever said such words about her before. Her—a beauty? With her skinny limbs and wild hair and skinned knees? She found herself smoothing her red velvet skirt and wondering if her collar was straight.

"Bertl, you are always so perfectly charming," the queen said, tucking her arm through his. "Now I must introduce you to my Minister of Education. . . ."

"Have you begun thinking about a husband for her?" Bertl asked the queen as she led him away. "I imagine that every prince alive will be fighting and clawing each other for the privilege. . . ."

As they walked off, Queen Veda cast a glance over her shoulder at Ana. Ana saw something in her eyes that she had never seen before.

It was fury, hatred.

ABOUT THE AUTHOR

NANCY OHLIN IS ALSO THE AUTHOR OF *BEAUTY*. BORN IN Tokyo, Japan, Nancy divided her childhood between there and Ohio. She received a BA in English from the University of Chicago, and lives in Ithaca, New York, with her family. Learn more at nancyohlin.com.